Hold Tight

Biker Daddy Bodyguards

Book 4

Sue Brown

Biker Daddy Bodyguards #4

Copyright ©2021 Sue Brown
Published by One Hat Press
This edition 2024
Cover design by Anna Martin

All Rights Reserved

*To Morticia Knight. This whole series is dedicated to you.
Thank you with all my heart.*

Blurb

Griff spends his evenings unofficially protecting the successful club owner, Jem Peacock, for the Biker Daddy Bodyguards. But Jem is a boy in need of a Daddy and Griff is desperate to take that job. He waits for Jem to trust him with the secret of his heart.

This young Daddy, all wiry muscle and compact strength, is not Jem's type. But when Jem's world implodes, Griff is the one by his side, guarding him, offering Jem the chance to explore his little side. Jem has longed for a special kind of Daddy, one who loves a femme little. Is he too old to have his dream? Can he trust Griff with his secret?

To his fellow bodyguards, Jem is a client. To their community, Jem is a boy in need of a special Daddy. To Griff, Jem is a little to be treasured. Will Jem give him that chance?

Chapter One

Jem

"Your bodyguard is here again," Max murmured, his amusement sparkling in his green eyes.

Jem Peacock didn't follow his brother's gaze. He refused to look over to the other booth in the VIP section of Peacock. He knew what he'd see. The bodyguard in question had been in their club every night for weeks.

"And this time he brought his friends with him. Mmmm, pretty." Max was practically salivating.

Jem held back a growl. "They're all loved-up, Maxy. Don't even think about it."

"Don't call me Maxy, *Jezza*. There's only one couple there. The rest are all big and burly. Yummy." Max licked his lips.

Jem rolled his eyes. "As I said, all loved up."

"Except your bodyguard, poor lamb. Sitting there all by himself. He looks so lonely."

"He's not my bodyguard." Jem scowled at Max's gleeful expression, but he kept his tone cool, knowing his brother would pounce on any sign of weakness. "And he's certainly not a lamb." There was nothing soft about Griff Carlton. He was all dark intensity and hard muscle. "He's not my type."

Max scoffed at him. "Oh, little brother, you can lie to yourself, but you can't lie to me. Griff is so your bodyguard. How many nights has he been in here since you met him?"

"I don't know." Jem glared at his brother, but it didn't take the wicked grin off Max's face, and Jem knew what he was going to say.

"Every night. Your boy has been here every single night for the past two months."

"He's not my boy." Jem held back a shiver. Griff may be years younger than Jem, but he was definitely *not* a boy.

"No," Max drawled. "He's certainly not your *boy*. Your Daddy, perhaps?"

"Enough," Jem snapped.

To his surprise, Max looked apologetic. "I just think you're being an idiot. This man is interested in you. You know that. I know that. He *really* knows that. Why are you refusing to see it?"

"You know why."

Max rolled his eyes. "So you have to kiss a lot of frogs before you find your one true Daddy. And now you've found him, Jem. He's sitting behind you, staring at you like you're his Kylie Minogue."

Jem wrinkled his nose at the analogy. He'd never understood his brother's passion for a diminutive Australian singer, but it had lasted a lifetime. Kylie was the only woman to whom Max would ever give his heart.

Max leaned forward and patted his hand. "All I'm saying is the gift horse is sitting behind you and he shouldn't be ignored. You deserve to be happy, little brother."

"I *am* happy," Jem insisted.

"Tell that to your face, because it doesn't seem to have gotten the message."

Jem had had enough. "I'm going to check on the kitchen." He strode away from Max, his brother's mocking laughter following him. He would not look behind him. He would not.

Max was like their grandmother's dog with a bone. He would gnaw on all Jem's weak spots until he exploded. Max knew that Jem wasn't interested in another Daddy. Two bad experiences were enough, and the last one had been humiliating. His last tentative dip into the Daddy world was how he'd met Griff in the first place. Jem had gotten himself entangled with an abusive Daddy, only he hadn't known it because he was rarely on the scene. He'd been flattered by Eric Strada's attention and had decided it was time he took the plunge back into the community again. That had ended abruptly when he'd gone to Romero's with Eric, only to be separated from Eric and escorted into Louis Romero's office. Jem had wanted the ground to open up and swallow him whole when he was told that, far from being interested in Jem, Eric was just desperate for anyone after being shunned by the community.

That had been one of the most mortifying moments of his life, then Griff had arrived to escort Jem home. He had frightened Jem at first. Raw power seemed to flow off him. But Griff had been sweet and kind, and a gentleman, seeing Jem to his door with nothing more than a good night.

Griff wasn't his type. He was too young, not even thirty. Jem preferred much older daddies, but now he was nearly forty and few Daddies would be interested in him. They wanted the sweet young twinks. Jem was sure he was too old and too damaged for the Daddies in the local community.

"I'm fine being on my own. I don't need anyone," he muttered as he headed to the kitchen.

You keep telling yourself that.

His brain was just as mocking as Max had been.

The kitchen staff looked up in confusion when Jem walked through the door. It wasn't that they weren't used to seeing him, but not generally during opening hours. Jem spent most of his time front of house, with Max dealing behind the scenes.

"Is everything all right, boss?" Ray, the sous chef, asked.

Jem huffed and squeezed the bridge of his nose before the pressure in his head threatened to become a full-blown headache. "Yes, just running away from my brother before I pop him on the nose."

He smiled, and everyone laughed. They were all used to the fractious relationship between the Peacock brothers. The two of them loved each other dearly, but they also rubbed each other up the wrong way. They were just careful to keep their real arguments in private.

"Any problems before I go?" he asked.

"Not today."

Jem nodded, and backed out of the kitchen, knowing his presence was just slowing the line down. He hesitated, not sure what to do with himself now. The club was busy, but it always was. Peacock was one of the most successful clubs in Seattle, with few real rivals, apart from Romero's. But there was no trouble, the staff were experienced, and Jem found himself hunting for something to do. He didn't want to go back to the booth where his brother was, because that would be tacit admission that he'd run away. Perhaps he could go sit in the office and relax for a while before he came out again.

"Jem, good to see you."

Jem looked up to see the tall figure of Louis Romero striding toward him shadowed, as always, by his bodyguard and Daddy, Craig Booker. Jem plastered on a fake smile and held out his hand.

"Louis, it's been a while." *Well, two months since you pointed out I was being used.* "How are you?"

Louis took Jem's hand and shook it firmly. He was an elegant man, always immaculately dressed, today in a Hugo Boss suit. Jem had its counterpart in his own closet. They had a very similar taste in clothes, but they were in the same business, at the peak of their game in the club scene. He noticed the bruising from the assault had faded from Louis's face and he looked less haunted than he had the last time they'd met. Jem smiled at Craig, who was dressed more conservatively but just as immaculate, and offered his hand. Craig was around Griff's age and adored his older boy. Jem couldn't help the flare of resentment at their obvious happiness when they had destroyed his by telling him what kind of man Eric Strada was.

"Business is booming," Louis said.

"It's been good," Jem agreed. "I'm surprised to see you here."

He meant because Louis was a workaholic and involved with his own club. He was surprised to see Louis's embarrassed expression.

"The Biker Daddy Bodyguards decided on a night out," Louis admitted.

"The...what?"

"That's what they call themselves."

"I don't," Craig muttered behind Louis. "It's a stupid name."

Jem narrowed his eyes. "A night out? Or did they come to be nosy?"

Louis swung around to face his Daddy. "You see, I told you he would know what you were up to."

"You weren't exactly subtle," Jem pointed out. "What do you want, Louis?"

Louis turned back to face Jem. "Griff's been worrying about you. So we all came to see what the problem was."

Craig made a choking noise. "You're not supposed to come out with it like that, boy."

"The mistake you make, Daddy," Louis's voice reeked of condescension, "is thinking we're stupid. Jem knows exactly why we're here, and he's pissed off. Which I would be, in his place."

Even Jem was taken aback at Louis's blunt words. "Well, yes."

Louis patted Jem's arm. "Just ignore them all. They've all been working too hard and needed a night out, so they thought they'd bug you and Griff. They want everyone to be as loved up as they are. You think our community is bad? You've never seen a bunch of bodyguards trying to play Cupid."

Despite his annoyance, Jem couldn't help but laugh. He was used to security interfering, but the idea of huge, grim-faced, booted and suited men playing Cupid to each other was funny.

"Why don't you come and sit with us?" Louis asked. "We haven't had a chance to gossip for months, and I could do with something other than listening to them talk shop. And Joseph is running late as usual. Cade is on tour, so that just leaves me. At least you and I can talk business."

Jem stared at him in horror. He couldn't think of anything he wanted to do less, but Louis's arm went around his shoulders and he found himself steered back to the VIP section, Louis talking a mile a minute about a new club on the scene, and Craig trailing behind them as usual. Jem shot Louis a suspicious look, but Louis just carried on talking.

He had to run away; he couldn't do this. Jem looked at his brother who was still sitting at the booth, begging him to rescue him, but Max just waved and gave him a wicked grin. Jem scowled at him.

Traitor!

Max's grin said everything.

Griff

"Your boy is running away," Quinn Ryder observed.

"He's not my boy," Griff snapped.

"He's so your boy," Mo drawled. "He's just in denial. We all know that."

Griff clenched his jaw. Why he had agreed to go on this evening out, he didn't know. It was bad enough that they'd suddenly decided to change venue and go to Peacock. As far as he knew they'd been going to Romero's for the evening. Quinn and Craig had treated him like he was part of the Biker Daddy Bodyguards when he'd said no, and no, and no again. Mo pointed out that saying no was like catnip to them, and he'd have done better to use his safe word. Griff was damn sure they wouldn't have listened to that either.

And then when they arrived, they made sure he was seated so he could spend the evening staring at Jem. The man was a study in elegance and beauty, just like his club. He was wearing a midnight-blue suit which set off his dark coloring and his hair was immaculately styled, longer than when Griff had first met him. He took Griff's breath away. He knew that Jem wasn't interested in him as a Daddy, which he'd found hard to bear, but he told himself it didn't matter. Maybe one day they could be friends instead. First, he'd have to talk to Jem, instead of lurking in the club.

He saw Jem storm off after a discussion with his brother, and every instinct made him want to run after him to check he was okay.

"You should go after him," Quinn said.

"You need to make sure he's all right," Craig added.

Mo rolled his eyes. "Jeez, boy, pull your finger out and go check he's okay before these guys bust their panties."

Fuck no. Griff wasn't going anywhere.

Louis huffed and stood, forcing Griff to slide out of the booth. "Come on, Craig, we'll make sure Jem is okay."

He glared at Griff, but Griff could see the smile playing around his lips. This was nothing more than posturing. Obediently Craig followed Louis out of the booth and Griff sat back down again.

He was skewered by two sets of eyes focused on him, neither of them looking happy. "What?"

"Why aren't you going after him?" Quinn demanded.

"Because he's not my client, and he's not my boy. Why would I go after him? He'd probably have me thrown out of the club."

Quinn rolled his eyes. "You've been here every night for two months. I think you're safe."

"He wouldn't throw you out if you had him on his knees," Mo said.

Griff scowled at Mo. "Why did you turn into one of these guys? You were the sensible one, and now you've become just like these idiots."

Mo shrugged. "If you can't beat 'em, join 'em, et cetera. I'm happier than I've ever been."

This was true. The lonely, surly bodyguard had been replaced with a man Griff was sure he'd never actually seen before. Mo smiled and laughed and was never happier than when Joseph was in his lap, or over his knees being spanked.

"Jem needs a bodyguard, and he needs a Daddy. You're the ideal man. You know that, otherwise you wouldn't have been here every single night," Quinn pointed out. "CDR won't pay your expenses forever."

Griff leaned against the back of the booth and tried to act unaffected. "I suppose there's no use in me pointing out that Jem actually isn't in danger anymore. Eric Strada is dead. Peacock has security of its own; they use CDR. There is no need for me."

"And yet here you are, mooning over him every night," Mo drawled.

"And charging it to the BDB account," Quinn added.

They both laughed at Griff's glower. The worst thing was, Mo was right. Griff had been dreaming about Jem since the day Griff escorted him home from Romero's. The delicate man entranced Griff, and he wanted to enfold him in his arms and protect him from the rest of the world. Griff had never felt like this about any client before. He was laid back, content to work his assignments and get on with his life. He ran with his dog, he rode his bike, and he loved life. But now he had tumbled head over heels for a man who didn't notice his existence. Jem never once looked his way. Griff hated that.

Suddenly that man was by the booth, and Griff forgot how to breathe.

"Move over, Griff," Louis ordered. "Jem and I want to talk shop."

Griff was damn sure that was the last thing Jem wanted to do, but he hadn't been given a choice. Griff obediently moved along the seat, and Louis pointed at Jem to go in next to him. Louis seemed oblivious to the scowls from both Griff and Jem, and he waited as if he fully expected them to obey. For a boy, he sure did give out the orders. Jem huffed and slid in next to Griff, and Griff noticed Jem was careful not to meet his gaze. Louis followed him, and Craig sat on the end. For a hard-nosed bodyguard, Craig seemed content to let Louis lead matters. He put his arm around Louis who snuggled in with a contented sigh. Griff couldn't help but feel envious of the way they'd mended their relationship after years apart.

A waiter came over to take their drink order. Griff noticed that Jem ordered a soda.

"Not drinking tonight?" Louis asked.

Jem shook his head. "I don't drink much. I always end up making bad decisions and paying the price. Now it's gotten to be a habit."

Quinn gave him an approving look. "It's a good habit to have."

Jem seem to flush under his praise, and Griff wished he'd been the one to put the color there. It was torture sitting next to Jem, who had gotten involved in a long conversation with Louis about... Griff wasn't sure what they were talking about, and he didn't really care. He could feel the heat of the man against him. He wanted to take Jem away from here and show him what it was like to have a proper Daddy, not one that was an abuser.

"What did that beer mat ever do to you?" Mo drawled in his ear.

Griff looked at the small heap of paper in front of him. He'd shredded one of the paper coasters. "I didn't notice."

"We realize that." Quinn quirked a smile at him. "We asked you a question."

Griff felt his cheeks warm, but he answered as coolly as

he could. "I didn't hear that either. What was the question?"

"Are you going back to your usual gig at the end of your vacation?"

Griff gave him a steady look. "I'm sure you already know the answer to that."

"When I asked Dominic, he said you hadn't made a decision."

"I haven't." Griff had taken an extended vacation because he'd been burned out. But now he needed to get back to work. "I've been there a long time, and I think I need a change. The guys I usually work with have all left, and I'm not sure I want to start again with a new team."

"Are you thinking of leaving the security business?" Quinn asked.

Griff was suddenly aware that, beside him, Jem had stopped talking. He seemed to be waiting for Griff's answer. "I thought about it," he admitted honestly. "But I don't know what else to do. I've only ever worked in security. I thought about going back to school and studying to do something else, but I don't know what to retrain as."

"You could join us," Craig suggested.

Again, Griff was aware of the tension in the man next to him. As if he was expecting an answer.

"I could," Griff agreed. "But surely there's a limited need for bodyguards with our skill set."

"You'd think so, wouldn't you?" Mo said. "But business keeps rolling in."

"We are expanding outside Seattle now," Quinn added. "The clusterfuck Strada left us with reminded us that boys need protection too. Leo in San Francisco has asked us to recommend Daddy bodyguards who could set up business there."

"Is that guilt or forward thinking?" Griff asked.

"A bit of both. But we are looking for Daddies who we know and could recommend."

Griff stared at them. "You want me to move to San Francisco and set up Biker Daddy Bodyguards there?"

Beside him, Jem was rigid. He seemed not to like the way the conversation was going.

But the idea of moving to San Francisco was deeply appealing to Griff. He hadn't had the chance to travel much with CDR, as he'd been with the same company for a long time in their Seattle headquarters. He could start afresh somewhere, with a new Daddy community. Maybe find his own boy. But if he did that, he wouldn't be with the man beside him. Dammit, why did he have to fall in love just as he had the chance for a fresh start?

"Wow, how exciting," Louis said. "I love San Francisco, although I've only been there once. Once I opened the club, the chances to travel became few and far between."

"They could do with good men guarding their backs." Quinn grimaced. "Leo said they're in a mess. More and more boys are coming out of the woodwork, especially now Strada is dead. I'm sorry, Jem, for talking about him."

Jem shrugged. "It's all right, really. He didn't get a chance to hurt me. I was more mortified at not knowing what he was really like."

Griff turned to him. "I'm really glad he didn't get the chance to hurt you."

The table went silent, and Jem's eyes went wide. Griff suddenly realized what he'd said. "I mean—"

"It's okay," Jem said. Color spread across his cheeks. "Thank you. And thanks for taking me home that night."

"You're welcome," Griff said quietly.

Their gazes locked for a long moment.

Chapter Two

Jem

The Daddy of his dreams had potentially gotten a new job. Hundreds of miles away. Wasn't that the way Jem's luck always went? He was undoubtedly one of the unluckiest men in love. Even his brother, whose love life worked on the 'treat them mean, keep them keen' philosophy, had more luck than he did. His squeezes kept coming back for more.

Jem talked politely to Louis until he couldn't take any more, then he apologized and said he had to work. He couldn't cope with the gorgeous Daddy next to him, so close. Jem wanted to curl up in Griff's lap and let him take the loneliness away. Because that's what he was. So fucking lonely. Almost forty and nothing to show for it. All his contemporaries were in relationships, even Louis now. Jem had nothing and no one to call his own.

As he slid out of the booth, he caught Griff's miserable expression. The guy didn't seem pleased to see him leave. Or maybe he was just imagining it. Max was convinced that

Griff was interested in him. Why would he keep coming back to the club? But Griff hadn't made a move on him. Not once. Not even to offer him a drink. Maybe he just liked the club. Although Jem wasn't sure about that, either. Griff spent most of his time nursing one drink and then he'd leave. Jem had no idea what to think. But he couldn't sit there with Louis and the Daddies, pretending he wanted to be there.

Max had disappeared, so Jem did a slow circle around the club checking everyone was happy. It was a busy night but there was no hint of trouble, which he appreciated. Customers were drinking, dancing, and generally having a good time. So why did Jem feel so miserable in his own club? Peacock was his home. He should feel happy here.

"Jem?"

Jem stopped breathing. He turned to see Griff smiling at him. He'd forgotten just how big Griff seemed next to him, dominating the space around them.

"Hi." Jem couldn't think of what else to say.

Griff seemed equally dumbstruck. Then he took a deep breath. "Listen, would you have a drink with me?"

"Me?" Jem asked stupidly.

Griff's lips twitched. "Yes, you, if you want to."

"Why?"

Griff looked a bit confused at his question. "Because I like you."

Jem's next question was going to be "Why?" again, but he heard a voice say, "That's an excellent idea. Why don't you take the rest of the night off, Jem? I can manage here."

Jem was going to kill his brother. Slowly, painfully, and with whatever implement he had to hand. The smirk on his brother's face was enough to make him seethe. What if he didn't want to have a drink with Griff? Okay that really was stupid. Of course he wanted to have a drink with Griff.

Griff was still staring at him intently. Jem knew that if he said no, Griff wouldn't press him. Griff was a Daddy, a true Daddy, if his reputation in the community was accurate. Jem had done his own investigations into the man who had escorted him home. Griff would walk away because he was too much of a gentleman to force Jem into doing anything he didn't want to. So the ball was in Jem's court.

Jem ignored his brother and smiled at Griff, pleased to see Griff relax a fraction. "I'd like that, but not here. Otherwise my brother and half the bodyguard community will be interfering."

"I never interfere," Max spluttered.

"Did your nose just get bigger?" Jem asked sweetly.

Griff chuckled at Max's outraged expression. "I know where we can go where we won't meet anyone we know."

"You take care of him," Max said, his voice suddenly hard.

Jem rolled his eyes. "He's taking me for a drink, not putting me in chains in his dungeon."

He heard Griff's intake of breath. Well, well, well. That was unexpected. Maybe he did have to worry.

But Griff turned to Max. "Let me give you my number. You can check in with me as well as Jem. And my co-workers will vouch for me."

"I know who you are," Max said. "I've already checked you out."

"Max!" Jem was outraged, even though he'd done the same thing.

"Gotta make sure you're safe, little brother." Max grinned at Jem's eye roll.

"Peacock isn't the wild west, Max," Jem groused.

"You never know." There was something in Max's expression...Jem didn't know what it was, but he didn't understand it.

But before he could question his brother, Griff just nodded as if being investigated was an everyday occurrence. "Good, then you'll know I've worked for CDR for many years. I've lived in my apartment for five years, and I have a dog."

Max groaned. "Did you have to say the d word?"

Griff looked confused. "D word? Do you mean dog?"

"What kind of dog?" Jem asked eagerly. "How old is it?"

"You mean you didn't find out when you were doing your own investigations?" Griff teased.

Jem frowned. "No. That was left out of the report. I'm going to have a word with my security on that." Then he realized he'd just admitted he had also checked out Griff. "Oh."

"Next time you want information on me, just ask Quinn or Craig. Or even Louis. Mo will tell you to fuck off."

"Oh God, why did I ever think you were a good idea for my brother?" Max said.

Griff raised an eyebrow. "I have no idea."

"Let's get out of here," Jem suggested. He could see Quinn and the guys looking over, and he knew that in a moment he and Griff would be surrounded by huge gossips who wanted to interfere even more than his brother did.

Griff looked over his shoulder and obviously came to the same conclusion, because he grinned at Jem. "Let's go."

"Cowards," Max muttered.

Jem flipped his brother off, and they headed toward the back of the club, where it was quiet and not full of people who wanted to meddle in their relationship. Not that they had a relationship. Yet. Not that Jem wanted to even think about that. He couldn't afford to get invested, if Griff was going to move away.

"I need to get my jacket from my apartment," Jem said.

"You obviously live upstairs. Where did you have me drive when I took you home from Romero's?"

"It's Max's place," Jem confessed. "It has scary Herman on the door, and I was worried Eric might turn up here after you threw him out of the club."

"That was sensible."

Jem wanted to hug Griff's approval to him.

"I'll wait for you here," Griff added. Jem paused and Griff looked concerned. "Is everything all right, Jem?"

"Are you sure you want to go out with me? I know everyone is sticking their nose in where it's not wanted."

Griff's smile was gentle. "I want to take you out for a drink, but not where everyone else is. Much as I love my co-workers, you know what they're like."

"I do. Peacock has worked with CDR since they first started, but this is the first time I've seen so much of them."

"Go get your jacket, and we'll escape." It was an order, albeit a gentle one.

Jem obeyed, running up the stairs to the private apartment where he lived. Once upon a time the whole family had shared the apartment, but now his parents were dead, and Max preferred to live off-site. Jem had never found anywhere else he'd wanted to be.

He grabbed his coat and scarf, and took one look at himself in the mirror. He was relieved to see he looked immaculate as ever, and not the hot mess he felt inside his head.

Griff was where he'd left him, and yes, that had been a worry too. Jem knew he had no self-esteem when it came to men. His track record had proved how disastrous he was at picking guys, let alone a Daddy.

"I'm ready," he said. He noticed that Griff was now wearing a leather biker jacket. "Are we going on a bike, because I'm not really dressed for it."

Griff shook his head. "No, it's just the first jacket I picked up. My car is around the corner. Is there a back exit, so we don't have to face the peanut gallery?"

Jem grinned. "There is. You know they'll be disappointed if we don't go past them."

"They can be disappointed," Griff said flatly.

Oh, he liked this man. Jem warned himself that he was on a slippery slope. He couldn't afford to like Griff. But Griff placed a hand on Jem's lower back as they walked out of the club into the chilly night air. Jem felt protected with the man next to him.

"Where do you want to go?" he asked.

Griff looked a bit embarrassed. "Would you mind if we went back to my place for five minutes? I need to let my dog out for a quick walk. We could go for a drink at a local bar near me. It's quiet and nothing special, but we're not liable to meet anyone from CDR or your world."

Jem hesitated for a moment, unwilling to put himself into a situation where he might not be able to escape. Griff seemed to notice his reluctance.

"Call your brother and let him know what you're going to do. You can stay in the car if you would prefer, but it's totally up to you."

Jem squared his shoulders. "No, I trust you."

Griff stopped, and turned to look at him. "You shouldn't trust me yet, boy. You don't know me. But I promise you're safe with me."

Jem nodded, because he was so desperate to be able to

trust someone. Why not this Daddy with eyes like they wanted to bring Jem home?

"I'd like to meet your dog," Jem said, as Griff drove the short distance toward his apartment. "What kind of dog do you have?"

"Doris is a rottweiler mix. I'm lucky that they let me have her in my building. Don't let her size and scars put you off. She is a big old love bug, but she can look scary at first."

Jem's first reaction was, *he has a rottie called Doris?* Then, "Why does she have scars?"

"Her previous owners tried to use her in dog fighting," Griff said grimly.

"Poor baby," Jem murmured. "What a horrible thing to happen."

"I rescued her. She's no beauty, but all she wants is to be loved."

"Why did you call her Doris?"

"After Doris Day? She sings a lot. You'll understand that when you meet her."

Jem smiled at the thought. It had never occurred to him that Griff would have such a soft heart. "What do you do when you're working?"

"She stays with my neighbor, who spoils her rotten. Rob works from home and loves having company. Doris has got two big old gay guys waiting on her every whim."

Jem felt a touch of jealousy. "Rob?"

"Yeah. Rob and I have known each other for years. He used to be in security before he discovered he could write books and make a lot more money."

"You two aren't together?" Jem felt embarrassed about asking the question, but he didn't want to get involved in a threesome. He was strictly a one Daddy boy.

Griff laughed. "No way. Rob is a Master, not a Daddy or a boy. He's into much heavier shit than I ever would be."

Jem breathed a little easier. He could live with that.

Griff

It hadn't occurred to Griff when he'd been telling the story of his wonderful gay neighbor just how that might have sounded to Jem. But he was happy to reassure Jem there was nothing between him and Rob.

Rob was one of his best friends. Griff should be more worried that Rob would be into Jem.

"Here we are."

The apartment had an underground parking lot, and he quickly pulled into his assigned space. He turned to Jem. "You can stay here if you want. If you get worried you head straight for those stairs and they lead you to street level." He pointed in the direction of an exit sign.

"Are you like this all the time?"

Griff was confused. "What do you mean?"

"You keep giving me exit strategies. Are you like this with every man you meet?" Jem didn't sound annoyed, but he did sound, what, exasperated?

"It's my job to create exit strategies. It's what I do for work," Griff admitted. "But when I meet a new boy, his safety is paramount to me."

"Thank you," Jem said quietly. "I haven't had the best of experiences. I'm just not used to someone making such an effort, especially on a first date." Then he looked panicked. "Not that this is a date. I mean—"

"I hope you'll think of it as a date by the time I take you home," Griff said, pleased to see some of the fear ease in Jem's eyes. "If I do anything at all that worries you, then tell me." Griff was very insistent about this with everyone he met, client or boy. He was a man with a scary skill set, although Jem probably didn't know everything about that yet. But he knew he could be intense, and if anyone told him they were nervous about him, he was always willing to dial it down. "Do you still want to meet my dog?"

Jem gave him a brilliant smile. "I can't wait."

Griff lifted his hand as they stood outside his apartment door. "Hold up."

Jem look confused but he nodded.

"Doris, Doris, Doris?" Griff sang.

Silence. Then there was an answering howl.

"Doris, Doris, Doris?"

Ohoooooooooooooooooooooo!

Griff grinned at Jem. "Brace yourself."

He opened the door and immediately a solid black and tan dog leaped into his arms, frantically licking his face. Griff knew it was impossible to get away from the slobbery tongue, so he just let Doris greet him. Then Doris noticed he wasn't alone. She wriggled frantically, and he put her down. But he didn't allow her to leap up at Jem. Instead he pointed to the floor, and she planted her butt on the ground, still wiggling.

"Jem, meet Doris. Don't bend down to greet her just yet. Otherwise she will do the same to you. Doris, you stay there. This is a friend."

"What if I hadn't been a friend?"

"Then I'd tell her to eat you." At Jem's alarmed look, Griff smirked. "It wouldn't make any difference. She'd lick you to death whether you were friend or foe. She's a useless guard dog."

"Can I say hello to her now?" Jem begged.

Because Doris had waited obediently, and Jem was

giving him huge puppy dog eyes, Griff nodded. "Just remember it's not my fault if you get slobbered on."

To his shock Jem knelt in front of Doris. "Hello, girl," Jem crooned. "You're so beautiful, yes you are. What a beautiful girl." He scratched Doris behind the cauliflower ears. Her eyes closed and she rolled over to expose her belly to him.

Griff sighed. She really was an utter tart. "I've lost my dog."

He maneuvered them so he could now shut the door. "I just need to feed her and take her down to go potty. Then we can go for a drink."

"Or we could stay here and love on your dog," Jem suggested.

Griff furrowed his brow. "Are you sure? I didn't bring you back here for that. I really only need five minutes to feed her and take her for a quick walk."

"I spend my life in clubs and bars. I love the idea of spending time with your dog instead. I don't work the sort of hours where having a dog is possible," Jem said. "Please can we stay here?"

"If that's what you want. Just message your brother to tell him what you're doing and give him the address."

Jem scowled at him. "I'm nearly forty, Griff. I'm quite capable of spending an evening with a man without needing my brother's help."

Griff just gave him a long look. He could wait.

The stand-off grew painful but finally Jem looked away. "If you insist."

"I do. Just for tonight."

Griff dropped the subject then and whistled for Doris to come into the kitchen with him. Doris rolled over and got to her feet with a huff. Most days she tore straight into the kitchen, begging for her food, but obviously Jem was more of a distraction this evening.

Jem followed the two of them into Griff's tiny kitchen. Griff filled Doris's food bowl with kibble and set it down on the floor next to the water bowl.

"How long have you had Doris?" Jem asked.

"Five years. I had to move when I rescued Doris, as my previous apartment didn't allow animals. I was lucky to find this place. The owner is dog crazy and allows pets. It's a dump, but I don't need much. I'm either working or walking Doris."

"I envy you," Jem admitted over the sound of Doris eating noisily.

"Envy me?" Griff furrowed his brow. "Why?"

"You seem very content with your life. You have a dog, a good friend next door, a job you like doing."

Griff had never thought about it like that, but he was content with his lot. He would have liked a boy on a permanent basis, but he had never found the one. "I am happy. What about you?"

Jem looked away, not able to meet his gaze. "I love the club."

"Are you trying to convince me or yourself?"

"The club was my parents' dream. Then when they died, Max and I took it over. There was never any question that we would do something else."

"What would you like to have done?"

Jem shrugged. "It doesn't matter. It's never going to happen."

"Tell me," Griff insisted.

"I thought I'd find my Daddy and become a boy, 24/7. I had enough money to support myself. I wouldn't be a burden. I just wanted to be someone's boy." The words came out in a rush as if he was trying to justify them to himself.

Griff hesitated and then he said, "Your first Daddy, he abused you?"

Jem nodded.

"And you haven't had a relationship with anyone until Strada?"

"That was hardly a relationship," Jem snarled. "I was flattered that he paid me attention. I'm an old man, and someone actually wanted to talk to me."

Griff stepped up close to Jem, his heart squeezed by the pain in Jem's expression. He raised his hand very slowly so as not to spook him, then caressed Jem's smooth cheek with his thumb. "I want to do more than talk to you."

Chapter Three

Jem

Jem wrapped his hand around Griff's wrist. He wasn't sure whether he wanted to tug Griff's hand away from his face or keep it there. "Don't play with me," he pleaded. "I don't think I could take it for a third time."

"I'm not playing with you," Griff said.

Jem wanted to believe him, but he couldn't, not after his experiences with his previous Daddies. "You've only just met me. You don't know me."

"I want to get to know you. I want to be your Daddy."

"Why?" Jem demanded. "You could have a sweet twink who you could train, rather than an old man."

"You're not an old man. And I don't want a sweet twink. I want you."

Jem snorted. "No one wants a boy like me."

Griff frowned at him. "Are you telling me what I like, boy?"

Jem thrilled to Griff's stern tone, even as he bent his

head. He wanted so much to lay his head on Griff's shoulder and ask this Daddy to take care of him. But he was nearly forty, not five, and he couldn't let go.

"I'm just saying you should look elsewhere. I'm not the right boy for you."

Griff took Jem's hands in his and placed them over his heart. "I know you're scared, and I know you've got no reason to trust me, but at least listen to what I have to say."

"That's what frightens me. I do trust you, and I shouldn't. Not yet."

"You're right, you shouldn't trust me yet. But I hope in time I can earn it." Griff brushed his lips over Jem's knuckles.

Jem gave a helpless laugh. "You're saying all the right things."

"But you can't believe I mean them. I understand. Jem, be honest with me. You're longing for a Daddy, aren't you?"

Jem nodded, his lips twisted into a sad smile. "It's like this frantic need has built up inside me. I thought Eric could fulfil that need, but that didn't happen. What am I going to do, Griff? I can't go on like this. I've ignored it for so long now, it's burning inside of me."

He suddenly felt a nudge at his knee and looked down to see Doris staring up at him with longing eyes. He gave a shaky laugh and bent down to scratch her behind the ears. Her eyes closed in ecstasy. "You're very lucky, Doris, to have such a wonderful Daddy. I can see how well he takes care of you."

"She's the best recommendation I have," Griff said with a chuckle. "But you need to talk to other humans about me. Doris is biased."

"I'd take her opinion over most humans," Jem admitted.

"Nevertheless, you need to talk to Quinn and Craig

about me. And I can give you the phone number of my last boy."

"Why did you separate?" Jem asked.

"Lee got transferred to Paris for a long-term assignment. We talked about me going too, but in the end, we realized that our relationship wouldn't last, and we went our separate ways. I'm still friends with him, and I introduced him to his current Daddy."

Griff had been sad to see Lee go but he had been friends, rather than lovers, with Lee. They had both admitted it had been convenient rather than an affair of the heart. Sometimes he regretted not moving to Paris, but it had been the best decision in the end.

"You're very lucky to still be friends with him," Jem said.

Griff knew that, and he'd never regretted his relationship with Lee. "I think you'd like him. He's in his fifties, and his current Daddy is just thirty."

He saw Jem's eyes widen. "Not all of us prefer young twinks. Look at Craig and Louis. They've been madly in love since the day they met."

"And look what happened to them," Jem pointed out.

"They didn't communicate and split up. But now they're madly in love again, and I don't think Craig is ever going to let Louis out of his sight."

"Maybe." Jem didn't sound convinced.

But Griff knew Craig and Louis well enough to know that their second time together was the final time. "All I'm asking is for you to give me a chance to satisfy your boy. You don't have to give me your heart."

Was there an unspoken 'yet'? Jem didn't dare hope for that. He gave a short nod. "What do you propose?"

"Why don't we have a session together to see if we fit?"

It was just one session. Jem could do that. But he was so nervous. Jem desperately wanted a Daddy to see him for what he was. Why was he turning Griff away when the man was offering him all he'd ever wanted?

Jem took a deep breath and stepped off the edge of the cliff. "I'm free most afternoons. But you're probably working, aren't you?"

"At the moment I'm taking a vacation. What about tomorrow?"

God. Yes. No. Yes.

"Okay," he said, his voice cracking.

Griff's expression was gentle and kind. "We'll take this slowly, Jem."

Jem sucked in a deep breath. "If I agree to this...this arrangement, it's on a trial basis only." He wasn't going to give Griff anything more than that. He was an adult, and he was going to behave like one. Griff didn't need to know that Jem was doing his usual thing of tumbling helplessly for the first man to show him the slightest bit of affection.

Griff nodded. "Just the one session. No more commitment than that."

Jem tugged his hands away from Griff's and knelt on the floor to love on Doris again, needing the uncomplicated affection from her. "Do you want to go for a walk, Doris? Is that what you need?"

Above his head, Griff sighed loudly. "It's bad enough I lost my dog's heart to the man next door. Now she's falling in love with you."

Jem looked up and grinned at him. "Typical female."

"I don't know much about them," Griff admitted ruefully.

"You've never had a girlfriend?"

Griff shook his head. "My first relationship was as a Daddy to a thirty-five-year-old boy. I was eighteen."

Jem stared at him. "You went in feet first."

"Iggy trained me to be a Daddy. It was the best training I could have had. He was a nightmare, but I knew once I could manage him, I could manage anyone. We were together for two years."

"What happened to him?"

"He fell in love. I was devastated at the time, but it was so obvious the man he adored was right for him."

Jem suddenly felt rather sorry for Griff. "You've had a history of stepping back for people to go and do something different."

Griff gave a wry chuckle. "You noticed, huh?"

"What about taking what *you* want? Have you ever wanted to do that?"

"I think that's what I'm doing now."

Jem flushed as he suddenly understood Griff's pointed look. *He* was what Griff wanted, and Griff was ready to go after him. "Yes, well, should we get your dog walked?"

"Nice deflection," Griff teased.

"You noticed, huh?" Jem echoed Griff's words from earlier.

As if she understood, Doris gave a howl of approval, and they both chuckled.

"I think Doris agrees," Griff said.

He reached for Doris's leash and gave it to Jem. "Let's go then."

"You're picking up any poop," Jem warned him as he clipped the leash on the dog. Much as he liked Doris, he wasn't ready to start cleaning up after her.

Griff tsked in disapproval. "I see. You want all the fun, but I get to do all the dirty work."

Jem raised an eyebrow. "She is your dog," he pointed out. "You're her daddy. You're supposed to take care of her."

He sucked in a breath. Maybe Griff could be Jem's Daddy too and take care of him.

Unaware of Jem's frantic thoughts, Griff grumbled as he herded them both out of the door. Jem couldn't stop grinning as he followed Doris down the hall. She seemed to know where she was headed. He couldn't remember the last time he'd had so much fun. He didn't know where this thing with Griff was leading, but he wasn't about to leap fences.

Baby steps, Jem Peacock. Just one step at a time.

Griff

Griff saw the joy on Jem's face and reveled in it. It was so different from the tight, pinched look of earlier. He knew Doris had that effect on people, but he hoped some of it was to do with him, too. He let Doris lead the way, knowing his dog loved taking the same route every night.

"Doris is a stop and sniff dog," Jem observed.

"She's determined to sniff out all the neighborhood gossip. In the morning we go for a run, but at nighttime I let her lead me."

"Max wouldn't believe me if he could see what I was doing now." Jem chuckled.

"Doesn't he like dogs?"

"Max doesn't like anything that sheds, including humans."

Griff laughed at Jem's sour tone. "I've met a few clients like that. I've also introduced some of them to Doris, and they've melted over her. She has that effect on people."

"Don't expect that from Max. My brother has a heart of stone where pets are concerned."

"I'll take that into consideration," Griff said solemnly. And then smirked at Jem.

They wandered the streets, the residential area quiet around Griff's home. It was one of the reasons he'd picked the place. That, and it was all he could afford at the time that would allow pets.

"Where do you do your sessions?" Jem asked suddenly.

"I have a room in the apartment. It's supposed to be the guest bedroom, and when I get an inspection, I have to remember to put all the toys away. Once I forgot, and I got a pointed question about whether I had children. The landlord likes pets, but he's not so fond of kids."

"What did you say?" Jem asked.

"I said my niece had visited."

"Do you have a niece?"

Griff laughed. "I do. But the youngest is four years younger than me and doesn't play with toys anymore. The landlord has actually met her, but I'm just hoping he doesn't remember. I've got three nieces and two nephews."

"Wow, is there a big gap between you and your siblings?"

"I've got two sisters who are over fifty. I was the menopausal baby. We all get on well despite the age gap."

"I've just got Max. He's bad enough by himself. I don't think there'll be any baby Peacocks making their way into the world. It's kind of sad that the line will die with us."

Griff nodded. "You don't want kids?"

"I've never thought it was something I would have. What about you?" Jem sounded curt and there was an edge of tension in his voice. Griff decided he would pursue that later.

"It's never been on my radar. I prefer dogs to actual children. I like my nieces and nephews, but they're a similar age to me. I'm just waiting for them to start having kids too. Then I can stuff them full of candy, get them all hyped up, and give them back at the end of the day."

Jem looked at him and laughed. "You're going to be the great-guncle from hell."

"I certainly hope so." Griff was positively looking forward to it.

Doris launched forward, taking Jem with her. Jem yelped, and Griff wrapped his arms around him.

"Sorry about that," he said, not letting go of Jem. "She can get a bit enthusiastic."

"Are you sure you just haven't trained your dog so that you can get your arms around men?"

"You got me. Doris is trained so that I can cuddle gorgeous boys. Will it work?" He waggled his eyebrows and Jem chuckled.

"Ask me later."

Griff noticed that Jem made no effort to get out of Griff's embrace, seemingly content to stay there, his head resting on Griff's shoulder while Doris snuffled disconsolately at their feet. A backfire made them both flinch. Jem sighed and took a step backward.

"Have we walked enough for Miss Doris? I could really do with that soda now or a coffee."

Griff nodded. "I think she'll cope. Let's get that drink. Coffee sounds like a really good idea. My couch?"

Jem sighed. "Sounds good. I'll probably fall asleep."

Griff took a chance, keeping his hand on Jem's lower back as he guided the boy back to his apartment. Jem didn't make any move to pull away, instead seeking Griff's comfort. The boy seemed starved for touch, which couldn't be right. He was in the club scene. He must be used to being hugged.

Back in the apartment, Griff palmed Jem a treat for the dog. "Make her sit."

But Doris was no slouch, and before Jem could say a word her butt was on the kitchen floor.

Jem snorted and offered her the biscuit. "Wow, she's so gentle," he marveled as she took the bone-shaped treat.

"You expected her to take your fingers too?"

"Well, yeah."

Griff chuckled. "Training. Doris was very enthusiastic at first. Once she understood I wanted to keep my fingers, we were good."

"And she got a lot of treats," Jem observed.

"Doris is a canny old girl," Griff agreed. "Sit yourself down. Do you want a soda or coffee?"

"Soda please. Dr Pepper if you have it."

"I do."

Griff heard Jem telling Doris what a beautiful girl she was. He smiled as he pulled two sodas out of the refrigerator. He trusted Doris's judge of character. There had been some men he'd brought back to the house that she hadn't liked, and she had ignored all attempts to make friends with her. Jem, on the other hand, she seemed to love straight away. Griff stood in the doorway and watched Doris, her head on Jem's thigh, rumble happily as he caressed her head.

"You know she's going to leave hair over your pants leg, don't you?" Griff said wryly. "She's not supposed to be on the couch."

"She didn't tell me that." But Jem didn't push her off and he carried on petting her.

Griff sighed as he handed Jem a can. "Do you want a glass?"

"This is fine." Jem popped the can and took a long chug of the soda.

Griff was fascinated by Jem's throat working as he drank. Even that he found erotic. He had to think about something else before he popped a boner in front of Jem. He didn't want Jem to think he was being pressured into doing anything he didn't want.

He perched on the edge of the couch because Doris took up most of the space.

Jem grinned at him. "You could just move your dog."

Griff glanced at Doris who had her eyes closed and was snoring, obviously content. "Why would I do that? She's happy. You're happy." He laughed at Jem's almost shocked expression.

"Me?"

Griff nodded. "You're happy with Doris loving you, aren't you?"

Jem's hand paused. Doris opened one eye and gave a discontented rumble. Jem quickly apologized and started to pet her again. She smiled and her eyes closed.

"She's an attention whore," Jem said.

"She is."

"Doris is very lucky...to have you."

Griff noticed Jem had avoided answering the question about whether he was happy. "It's mutual. I rescued her and spoiled her rotten, and she made me part of her family." He hoped Jem understood what he was trying to tell him.

Jem huffed. "You think I need to be rescued?"

"I notice you focus on that part, and not being spoiled rotten and being made part of the family."

"It's hard not to feel like I'm some project you're taking on."

Griff moved so that he could sit back in the couch. Doris

grumbled at him for moving her butt, but he ignored the rumbles of discontent.

"What are you? As a boy, I mean."

"I think I'm a little, but I haven't really explored it with anyone yet."

Griff was pleased that Jem didn't pretend not to know what the question meant. "I have toys for littles. I have toys for most age ranges. And binkies and diapers. We can explore your needs." He saw Jem's eyes widen.

"Most Daddies I've met seem to prefer littles."

"Let's ignore most Daddies. I want you to focus on me." Griff knew there was the slightest edge to his voice, and from the way Jem's eyes narrowed, he'd spotted it too. "You don't have to be anything you don't want to be. If you think you're a middle, we can explore that too."

"What if we do the session, and you decide you don't like me?"

Griff thought it would be a cold day in hell before he decided he didn't like Jem Peacock, but Jem looked deadly serious, so he gave the question his consideration.

"We'll sit down and evaluate at the end of the session. If either of us decides it's not right, then we'll go our separate ways. No harm done. It will be a simple play session. Nothing beyond that. Definitely no sexual element. I just want to see you in boy mode, and I want you to see if my Daddy suits you." He saw Jem give a shiver. "What's wrong? I can see something is bothering you."

"My first Daddy was like you. He seemed to be organized, and he promised we would take things slowly. And we did. Almost too slow. For months he restricted our sessions to fun play and play dates. And that was fine. I was in my twenties, and I didn't know what I was doing. I'd had a few training sessions, but I thought Tony was the real thing."

Griff had a feeling he wasn't going to like what was coming next. He knew he needed to know, and he couldn't go into any arrangement with Jem without more information. He wasn't prepared to have even the one session without this conversation, in case it triggered something in Jem.

"What did Tony do to you, Jem?"

"It wasn't him."

Chapter Four

Jem

Jem closed his eyes, remembering the day everything changed. He felt a sudden touch on his hand. He opened his eyes expecting it to be Doris, but it was Griff.

"Tell me what he did." The order was clear even if his tone was kind.

"He arranged a play date with four other daddies. What I didn't realize was they weren't bringing littles." Jem stared at Griff bleakly. "I was the only little, and I was there to be shared around."

Griff stared at him in horror and Jem gave a shaky laugh.

"Yes, I see that expression a lot."

"Explain," Griff bit out.

"What I didn't understand was my Daddy wasn't interested in me sexually. He liked the playtime and the nurturing. He liked reading to me. He liked all the components of being a Daddy, but he didn't want to fuck me. And that was okay. I was starting to realize that. It was disappointing, but it wasn't the end of the world. But I didn't realize he would expect me to service other unattached Daddies to make up for it."

He could see the anger in Griff's expression, but when Griff spoke his tone was very mild.

"So you ended up being gang raped by four men?"

"People don't usually say that part out loud. They prefer euphemisms. But yes, they gang raped me while I was in little mode. It was a long time ago, Griff. I've gotten over it."

Sometimes he almost went a day without remembering.

Griff shook his head, his expression fierce. "No, you haven't, my...Jem. Let's not pretend you can get over something like that or minimize the damage it did to you. There's a reason you've been on your own for so long."

Jem looked over to the other side of the room rather than at Griff. He felt the weight of Griff's anger pressing down on him. He noticed a pacifier on one of the shelves. It had obviously been left there and forgotten about. Griff needed to be more careful if he wasn't going to attract unwanted questions from his landlord.

"What did you do?" Griff asked, breaking into his thoughts.

"I went home and called my brother. We agreed I couldn't call the police. Who the hell would've believed me, ten years ago? Who would believe me now?"

"You didn't tell anyone?"

"I said we didn't report it to the authorities. But Max knew who the guys were. He went straight to Graham Knight, and between them they made sure the five men were exiled from the community."

Jem looked at Griff. "There was a big fallout, and if it hadn't been for Max and Graham, I'm not sure I'd still be here. A lot of people blamed me at the time. They thought I overreacted. But Max and Graham supported me all the way."

"I'm glad they took care of you," Griff said. It was obvious he was trying to hold onto his control.

"After that, I decided to forget about my boy side forever. It wasn't something I needed to explore. At least, I thought that I could ignore it. We were remodeling the club, and that took up all my time."

"So when did you decide you needed more?"

"About the time Eric Strada asked me out," Jem said dryly.

"You really haven't had a chance to explore your boy side at all?"

Jem didn't realize he was digging his fingers into Doris until she grumbled. "I'm sorry, girl," he murmured. He smoothed out the ruffle in her fur and made sure she was happy again before he answered. "It's not something I ever thought I would come back to. I thought that the one experience had put me off forever."

"So what changed your mind?"

Jem blushed. "Someone escorted me home."

Griff smirked a little, but he said, "You said you'd been thinking about it around the time Eric Strada asked you out."

Jem huffed because this was going to sound stupid. "It was the Biker Daddy Bodyguards. They were so damn visible, and they made their boys so happy. They used to come to the club, and I watched them. They brought back feelings that I thought I'd forgotten about forever. I hated it," he admitted.

"You didn't want to be reminded of that aspect of your life."

"I put it behind me a long time ago, and now suddenly it was in my face."

"Have you talked to your brother about it?"

"He tried to get me back into the community a long time ago, so now he just finds it funny that the community is coming to me."

"He's not a Daddy or a little?"

Jem shook his head. His brother would howl with laughter if he could hear that question. "Max is...not fussy." He sighed at Griff's raise of his eyebrow. "Max isn't anything. He's not even vers. He likes sex, but he remains emotionally detached. He's the opposite of me."

"It's good to know. You are obviously close to your brother, and it would be difficult if he were opposed to your little side."

"I don't think he understands it. How can you, if you're not in the community?"

"What does he think about me? I assume he knows who I am?"

"He just wished you'd hurry up and get on with it. He wasn't sure why you kept coming to the club and not trying to approach me."

"Initially it was because I was worried about Eric Strada giving you trouble in the club," Griff admitted. "It wouldn't be the first time he's done that. But then we discovered Strada had killed himself."

"But you kept coming back."

Jem had been touched, and confused, by Griff's constant appearances. Griff didn't even seem to take much notice of him when he was in the club. Jem had authorized

Griff's VIP club membership even though he didn't qualify. He had never been worried about Griff's appearances. And that concerned him. He was worried he was putting his trust in somebody too soon, again.

Griff hesitated. "You noticed, huh?"

"You're kinda hard to miss," Jem pointed out dryly.

"I noticed my change in my membership. Was it you?"

"I figured if you were going to guard me, you could at least do it close to me."

"There's something else you need to know," Griff admitted.

Jem had a sinking feeling he knew exactly what Griff was going to say. "Which one of them made you do this?" he asked harshly, regretting now he'd ever thought Griff was interested in him. Why was he always such a fool to believe men could find him attractive? He was a loser.

"Whatever's going through your head, you can get rid of it now, boy. No one put me up to this. I like you," Griff enunciated clearly. "I've had more trouble trying to keep them away from the club. You know what they're like for interfering."

Anger was still coursing through Jem when he suddenly realized what Griff had said. "No one asked you to guard me?"

"I know CDR does the club security, and the guys you have working for you are good men. Professionals. But I wasn't so sure about you."

Jem winced at his implication.

Griff continued, obviously not realizing what he'd said. "I was worried about you, and I didn't trust Eric Strada not to come back. He was trouble with a capital T. I was on an extended vacation and had some time to spare."

"You spent a fortune in my club to make sure I was all right?"

Griff looked embarrassed as he admitted, "I confess that I put all the expenses through CDR. No, they didn't put me up to it, but your club is pricey. Way out of range for a poor bodyguard like me. CDR can foot the bill."

Jem snorted at him. Doris opened one eye, decided everything was all right, and went back to sleep. "It's supposed to be pricey. We only want to attract the top clientele."

Griff gave him a solemn nod. "I know. You want to attract people like me. I've got a VIP membership, you know."

They grinned at each other, and Jem realized he hadn't had a banter like this with anyone except his brother for so long. He didn't have many friends outside the club. After being raped, he had retreated inside and didn't trust anyone beyond his brother. Max had been like a whole family to him, understanding his needs when his parents didn't. He considered himself lucky to have Max. But maybe he'd found another friend now. Someone who understood him just as well, maybe even more.

"I'm glad we had this discussion now," Jem admitted. "There's something else I need to know."

"You can ask me anything you like. In fact, the more questions you ask me, the better. I don't want there to be any secrets between us. I will always give you a truthful answer, even if that's not the answer you want to hear."

Jem thought about that for a minute before he asked his question. He knew his self-esteem was fragile and he wasn't sure he could take blunt honesty. But maybe that was better. If he heard the truth, he could take time to process it. Maybe Griff wouldn't mind that.

"I need to know if you like sex."

Griff

That was probably the last question Griff expected Jem to ask.

"Yes, I like sex. But I don't expect you to have sex with me if you don't want it."

"I want it," Jem said, "I just don't know if I can do it."

Griff chewed on the inside of his bottom lip and then asked the question. "Was the rape your only sexual experience?"

"No, but there was only a boyfriend before, and virtually nothing since. I struggle with the idea of anyone touching my body."

"Thank you for telling me that. We can start with me not initiating touching you. But you are welcome to initiate any contact with me."

Griff saw the relief on Jem's face. As more and more information was pulled from Jem, he realized that taking on this boy was going to be a whole bigger job than he'd ever considered. For a moment he wasn't sure he was up to the task. It was one thing to guard a boy from potential danger, but it was another to take on a boy who'd been as badly damaged as Jem had. He thought briefly of Quinn Ryder, his de facto boss at Biker Daddy Bodyguards. He'd taken on the care of Cade Connolly, only to discover the boy had been badly abused by his previous Daddy. He would be the better Daddy for Jem in this instance. But Quinn and Cade were in love, and nothing and no one would come between them. Cade would kill anyone who laid a finger on Quinn. Quinn always joked it was meant to be the other way around, but they all knew who held the power in their relationship.

"I want you to go home and think about it before you make any real decision," Griff insisted. He saw the mulish expression on Jem's face. "I know what you think you want, boy, but it's one thing to need it in your head, it's another to actually take that first step."

He was sure he heard a growl, but he was adamant that Jem needed to take time to think. If this was the first order he had to give his boy, it was the right one.

Jem huffed and subsided into the couch. Doris woke up with a discontented expression because Jem had stopped petting her, but once she realized she'd lost Jem's attention, Doris fell back to sleep.

"I think I'd like to go home now," Jem admitted. "I've got a lot to think about."

"That's a good idea," Griff agreed, telling himself not to be disappointed as he'd actually ordered Jem to go home. "I'll drive you."

Jem shook his head. "I can get a car."

"I will drive you home. I'm your Daddy. It's my responsibility to make sure you're safe." Griff infused his stern tone with a growl, pleased to see Jem shudder. Oh yes, his boy liked being told what to do.

"Before I go, please could I see the room you have for your boys? It's been such a long time since I was in a playroom."

Griff patted Doris's butt to get her to move. He ignored her outraged expression as he stood and held out his hand to Jem. "Of course you can, and you're welcome to make any suggestions that would improve your sessions with me."

Jem's hand was warm in his. Griff kept hold of it as he walked along the hall to his playroom. He opened the door and switched on the light, then stood back to let Jem go in. He heard Jem's gasp.

"It's so large."

"Originally this was the master bedroom, bathroom, and closet. But I don't need much in the way of sleeping space. What I really need is room to play with my boy, and the bathroom has a tub in it. I like bathing my boys. I'm really lucky to have this much space."

"I'd like to be bathed," Jem admitted, with a delicate blush. "How do you explain it to your guests?"

Griff shrugged. "I don't get many visitors. Those I do get are mainly people from the community, or from CDR, and they don't care. My family know who I am."

"They know you're a Daddy?" Jem's jaw dropped open.

"They do. It's not like they really understand, like Max, but once I explained that no, it's nothing to do with kids, and all to do with consenting adults, they relaxed. It also helps that all my boys were older than me. I'm not ashamed of what I do."

Jem bit his lip. "I am, sometimes."

"It's not surprising. You haven't really had a chance to explore your boy self. Take a good look around the room and tell me what you'd like to play with the next time you're here."

Jem went further into the room. Griff had laid out most of his toys on shelves. There were train sets and cars intermingled with dolls and tea sets. "Do you have sessions with girls?"

"No, never."

Jem looked relieved. "I had to check."

"Some of the boys liked playing with the dolls or having tea parties. Iggy used to like pretending to make cakes."

He watched Jem run a finger over the lace of one of the

dolls and filed that away to explore later. Maybe Jem had another side he wanted to explore.

"You can play with anything you want to, and anything you want me to add I can get."

"I like sucking on a binky," Jem said almost defiantly.

Griff went over to a drawer and opened it up. "Take your pick."

Jem's eyes went wide. "These are for adults."

"I have binkies and Sippy cups."

There was one other thing he wanted to show Jem. Griff walked into his closet and switched on the light. There was a full-sized changing mat. He saw Jem's eyes go wide.

"This is also something we can explore if you want."

It was as if the tension had drained out of Jem. He knew that Griff would supply his needs and not laugh at him, or think he was wrong.

"I wanted… But I wasn't sure I could ask."

"You can ask for anything you want to explore. I might not always say yes. I might not always think you're ready for things. But we can explore it together."

"I think I'd like to go home now, Daddy." Jem's voice was little, and Griff treated him accordingly.

He led Jem out of the closet, turned off the light and closed the door, ignoring Jem's wistful look. "Let's get your jacket, and I'll take you home."

Back in the main room, Griff helped Jem on with his coat and buttoned it up for him. Jem patted Doris, told her what a good girl she was, and said he'd see her soon. Doris rumbled happily.

Out in the street, Griff drove through the almost deserted streets of his residential area toward the club. "I'll pick you up tomorrow afternoon at two."

"Okay." Jem sounded almost breathy, excited.

"We'll talk again tomorrow before we do anything."

"I hope we're not just going to talk."

Griff shot Jem a quick look, seeing his disgusted expression. He chuckled and said, "No, we're not just going to talk. I promised you a session."

Jem sighed as they pulled up outside the club. There were still lines stretching around the block, waiting to get into Peacock. "Back to the real world."

"What time will you get to bed?" Griff asked.

"Six, maybe seven. It depends how long it takes to clear up."

"We can make the session later if you'd prefer."

Jem shook his head. "I don't sleep that much. Two o'clock is fine. What are you going to do?"

"I'm going back to my bed. Unlike you, I like my sleep. I have a session to prepare for in the morning."

Jem wrinkled his forehead. "You spent the last couple of months sitting in my club till three in the morning."

"It's nearly killed me," Griff admitted sheepishly. "But I've been on vacation, so I've been sleeping in till lunchtime most days."

"You'll soon get used to it," Jem assured him.

Griff was sure that he wouldn't, but he didn't want to argue with his new boy. His heart gave an excited leap at the thought. "I'll walk you to the door," he said.

"There's no need. Security is there."

Griff said nothing, but he went around to Jem's side of the car and opened the door.

Jem gave him a quizzical look. "This is one of those Daddy things, isn't it? I say everything is okay, and you ignore me."

Griff looked down into Jem's sweet face. "It's my job to

ensure that you're safe. And the only reason I'm not sitting in the club until three tonight is that I know there's a room full of CDR operatives who will be making sure you're fine."

Jem groaned. "You checked, didn't you? Before we left."

Griff just smirked.

Chapter Five

Jem

Jem wandered through the VIP section of the club, nodding at people he knew, and kissing one or two who approached him, their hands fluttering as they air-kissed him. Conchita was here tonight. She hadn't been here when he left. He would make sure she got star treatment. If it hadn't been for the highly strung, temperamental woman, Louis wouldn't have survived the assault in the back alley behind Romero's. Conchita had ensured herself top treatment in any club she chose in Seattle. She knew it, of course, and played on it, but no one minded. She was a queen and deserved to be treated as such. He went over to the bar and signaled to Elise, a slender, pretty, blonde bartender with a mind like a steel trap.

"Conchita is here tonight."

"Already noted, Jem," Elise assured him. "She's seated at her favorite table, and I've assigned Pierre to take care of her. She is already fluttering over his accent."

"Good. Have you any idea where my brother is?"

She furrowed her brow and then shook her head. "I haven't seen him for an hour, but we've been very busy."

That was odd. Max was always visible, if not front of house, then in the back.

"I'll go find him. He's probably snarling at the accounts."

Jem saw a man approaching him, and he sighed inwardly, knowing that Darius was probably about to complain he hadn't received VIP treatment. The man was a pain in the ass, but he was a loyal customer, and Jem didn't want to annoy him. It took fifteen minutes and all of Jem's attention to calm him down. But finally he was free to look for his errant brother.

He saw Quinn, Craig, Mo, and Louis, still chatting at the same table they'd been at before. He waved a hand at them as they acknowledged him. He could see the curious expression on Louis's face and knew he was going to get a call the next day. Now Joseph, Mo's new boy, was cuddled up next to him. He felt a sudden rush of jealousy, which was stupid because Griff had claimed him. Maybe next time he would be sitting there with Griff's arm around him. He also felt momentarily sorry for Quinn, who spent a lot of time apart from his lover and boy, Cade. He'd heard rumors that Quinn was supposed to be Cade's head of security, but that didn't seem to have happened.

Max wasn't in his office, and he wasn't in the kitchen. Jem started to have a niggling feeling in the pit of his stomach. His brother was very predictable and not being able to find him was concerning. Bearing in mind what had happened to Louis, Jem checked the back alley, which was fully lit. It was thankfully empty. The only other place he could think Max could be was upstairs in his apartment.

He called out as he went up the narrow staircase, but he

didn't receive any reply. As he reached the top of the stairs he saw a light coming from the main room. He relaxed, as he hadn't left a light on when he'd started work. Max had to be there.

"Maxy, what are you doing up here?" Jem went into the room, relieved to see his brother sitting on the couch, but Max didn't respond, not even to his hated nickname.

"Max, what's wrong?"

Max was splayed out on the couch, his head slumped and his eyes closed.

Fear shot through Jem. He rushed over, kneeling beside his brother, feeling for a pulse point at the base of his neck. It was weak under his fingertips, but Max was alive. Jem breathed a sigh of relief when he saw Max's eyelids flutter.

"You," Max groaned, one hand curling around Jem's bicep. "Need..." Max moved his hand and Jem stared aghast at the spreading red bloom on his shirt.

"What the hell happened?"

Max licked his lips, his breaths shallow. It was obviously an effort to speak. "Shot. You..."

"It's all right. I'll take care of you," Jem assured him. He looked around frantically for something to press against the wound.

"Why you..."

"Stop talking, Max."

In desperation, he wrenched off his shirt and pressed it into the wound, making his brother wince.

"Hurts," Max managed, gasping.

"Sorry, but I've got to stop the bleeding."

Fumbling one-handed for his phone, Jem dialed 9-1-1 for an ambulance. When the police and an ambulance were on their way, he called his security.

He wasn't surprised to hear thunderous footsteps

coming up the staircase within moments. He was even less surprised to see Quinn and his friends in the lead.

"What the fuck happened?" Quinn barked.

"Max has been shot," Jem said.

He found himself pushed to the side with Louis's arm around him as Quinn and Mo went to work on Max.

"Max, who did this to you?" Quinn demanded.

Max looked slowly around the room. He didn't seem to focus on Quinn's question. "Jem...you gotta..."

"Max," Quinn snapped. "Listen to me. Who did this to you?"

"Jem."

"I'm here, Max. I'm here." Tears filled Jem's eyes, and everything blurred.

"Come on," Louis urged. "Give them space to work."

"I can't leave Max. There's no one else except us." Jem couldn't control his shivers and wrapped his arms around himself. Max had stopped talking, stopped responding to Quinn's questions.

"I know, baby," Louis said soothingly. "We'll go into the kitchen. We won't be far away. The cops and paramedics will be here soon."

In the small kitchen, Louis made coffee for him. Jem took a sip from the cup Louis urged on him and nearly choked. It was full of sugar and creamer and tasted vile.

"Drink it all," Louis insisted. "You're in shock."

Jem just wanted to put it down the sink, but Louis stared at him until he drank more. It was disgusting that he felt more grounded after a few sips.

Once Jem had finished the coffee, Louis took the cup from him. "Have you called Griff?"

Griff. Jem had completely forgotten. He shook his head.

"Do it now, before the police arrive."

"I don't know where my phone is." Jem stared at his blood-stained hands as if they could provide the answers.

Louis pulled out his phone and tapped the screen.

Why did Louis have Griff's phone number? Jem gritted his teeth and told himself to get over it. His brother could be dying a few feet from him, and he was jealous of Louis.

"Griff, darling. Get your ass back to the club. There's been a shooting."

Jem could hear shouting at the other end.

"No, no. He's fine. It's his brother, Max. He's been shot."

Jem heard a distinct "Asshole!"

"He's on his way," Louis said as he disconnected the call.

Jem shuddered with relief. He knew once Griff was here, he'd be all right. "You know he's going to kill you for scaring him."

"Craig will protect me," Louis said confidently.

Jem thought Craig was more likely to put Louis over his knee for sassing Griff. But maybe that was what Louis called protection.

More footsteps sounded on the stairs, and the quiet voice of Mo directing them to Max. Five minutes later, a uniformed police officer, looking as if he was barely out of high school, appeared in the doorway.

"Mr. Peacock?"

"That's me," Jem said.

"Come with me," the cop ordered.

"My brother..."

"He's on his way to hospital," the officer said kindly. "As soon as you're finished with us you can go there."

Jem was hustled down to the club and into his office where he met a stern-faced, dark-haired, handsome detective sitting in *his* chair. Another guy in a suit sat on the couch by the window. The uniformed officer placed a chair facing the detective and left the room.

"Take a seat, Mr. Peacock," the detective growled.

Jem collapsed into it, not having the energy to protest.

The detective scowled at him. He reminded Jem of a TV policeman, but he couldn't remember which one. Jem had watched so many crime shows.

"I'm Detective Hamilton and my partner is Detective Ronson."

The other man nodded at Jem, but he kept silent, letting his TV cop sidekick bark out all the questions. Hamilton kept asking him questions Jem didn't know the answers to. It seemed to focus around the gun. Jem knew he had to be a suspect, but he kept telling them he didn't own a gun. He didn't keep any weapons on the premises. He employed security for that reason. He repeated the same things over and over until he was sick of saying them.

"You say Mr. Peacock was talking when you arrived."

"Yes," Jem said wearily. "He said my name several times, told me he was shot and that it hurt. That was all he said to me, before security arrived and took over."

Detective Hamilton curled his lip.

Jem wasn't interested in his opinions on security and bodyguards, but he was sure he was going to get them.

"When Ryder asked who shot him, he said your name. Why do you think that was?"

Jem stared at him. "I don't know. I thought he wanted to know I was still there. Maybe he was trying to tell me something?"

The detective opened his mouth but suddenly there was shouting, and then Jem heard someone say, "I'm sorry, sir, you can't come in here."

"Open the damn door."

Griff! Jem's head shot up at the familiar voice.

Hamilton eyed him shrewdly. "Who's that?"

"He's my... boyfriend." Thank goodness Jem hadn't stumbled over the word Daddy.

"I don't care who he is. He's not coming in here until we've finished our conversation."

Griff didn't burst through the door, so Jem assumed he had been moved away. Still, at least he was here. He came when he was needed.

"I was with him. I went to his apartment and met his dog." Jem saw Hamilton's eyebrows raise comically. "That's why I wasn't in the club when Max was shot. Griff offered to take me out for a coffee. He also works for CDR, the security team."

The detective sighed. "Of course he does."

Jem narrowed his eyes at the man's tone. "Do you know them?"

"Everyone knows CDR. They're assholes, but they get the job done." The grudging praise made Jem warm to Hamilton until he said, "Why do you think your brother kept saying your name?"

"I've already answered that. I don't know."

"Maybe he thinks you were the one who shot him."

"But I didn't. I found him."

The detective leaned back in the chair. "So you say." At Jem's shiver, he raised an eyebrow. "Are you cold, Mr. Peacock?"

"I'm scared that my brother is dying, and I'm stuck here answering your damn questions," Jem snapped, anger overtaking his fear.

Hamilton didn't seem moved by Jem's fury. "Not too

many more questions. You say your brother doesn't live with you?"

"No. He has an apartment downtown."

"So why would he be in your apartment rather than in the club?"

"I don't know," Jem snapped again, frustrated by the constant questions. "I told you this the first time you asked me. Max usually comes up to my apartment after the club is closed and we've cleared away. But not during opening hours."

Hamiton glanced at his partner and then looked at Jem. "We're done for now. You'll need to come down to the precinct tomorrow morning. We may have more questions."

"Do I need a lawyer?"

The detective gave him a hard look. "I don't know, Mr. Peacock. Do you?"

Griff

Griff was standing in his playroom, making tentative plans for the following day. Doris was at his feet leaning against him. He hadn't expected a phone call, and he frowned when he saw Louis's number.

"Louis?"

"Griff, darling. Get your ass back to the club. There's been a shooting."

Ice water flooded through Griff's veins. "Jem! Is he all right?"

"No, no. He's fine. It's his brother, Max. He's been shot."

Griff couldn't stop the explosive, "Asshole!"

He disconnected without another word and stared at the rottie. "I've got to go, Doris, my boy needs me."

Doris seemed to nod approvingly.

He drove the short distance to the club in a fiercely controlled manner. He wanted to put his foot down on the gas pedal, but people were spilling out from the clubs and onto the pavement.

There was tape across the entrance to the club and two cops stood there. He wondered how the hell he was going to gain access. He dialed Quinn's number.

"I'm outside," he said curtly.

"Leave it with me."

He didn't know what magic Quinn worked, but one of the cops beckoned him over. He was given booties and gloves and led through the club to the private area at the back. Quinn greeted him with a grim face.

"Jem is being questioned by the cops in his office. Max is going to the hospital. It doesn't look good."

Griff clenched his jaw. Jem would be devastated. He had one selfish moment of wondering if Jem would ever forgive him for taking him away from the club when his brother needed him. And in the next moment he was thanking God that Jem had been away from the club because otherwise he might be the one facing death. "Louis said he'd been shot? Have you got the CCTV footage?" Griff lowered his voice, knowing there were cops in earshot.

"Dominic is going over it now. We had to give it to the cops of course, but we've got a head start on them."

Griff knew this was a grim situation for CDR. Allowing one of their clients to be shot. But they were strong enough to be able to withstand a knock to their reputation. He really hoped Max survived, for Jem's sake.

"Where's Jem's office?"

Quinn pointed it out. "But you won't be allowed to go in there."

Griff nodded. "I know, but I just want Jem to know I'm here."

Quinn didn't argue, which Griff was thankful for, because he would have ignored him anyway. Griff approached the officers outside the door who told him he wasn't allowed to go in.

"Open the damn door." Then he said at a lower volume, "My boyfriend is in there."

The officer's eyes narrowed. "I don't care if your mother is in there, you still can't go in. Go back to the lounge area."

Griff did what he was told, satisfied as he returned. Jem knew Griff was here. That was all that mattered. Griff would wait all night if necessary, for Jem to come out of the room.

Quinn raised an eyebrow as he returned. "Do I need to soothe any ruffled feathers? Am I gonna get any angry cops on my ass?"

Griff shrugged. "You should be fine. I only annoyed them a little bit."

"Thanks." Quinn pulled a face. "Dominic insists I have to talk to the police now."

"You know he hates dealing with them. One asshole officer and Dominic is steaming."

"Why won't they let Jem be with his brother?"

"Max is going straight into surgery. They may as well get the questioning over and done with now. He was the one to find Max."

"Surely they don't think he shot his brother?" Griff demanded.

"Everyone's a suspect at this point. The door to the apartment was open. Anyone could have gotten upstairs." Quinn's expression hardened. "I'll be talking to the club security about how they missed the open door."

Griff clenched his jaw. He was ready to punch his fist through the wall in frustration.

Quinn squeezed Griff's shoulder, his expression softening. "I know this is hard, but let the cops talk to Jem now. By the time we get to the hospital, Max might be in recovery."

Griff took a deep breath and forced himself to calm down. "Where is Louis?"

"He was with Jem until the cops took him in for questioning, but now I think he's with Conchita. The cops were relieved when they found somebody who could calm her down. She's...uh...lively."

"Who's Conchita?" Griff asked.

"Conchita is the wonderful woman who saved my boy," Craig said as he joined them.

Quinn rolled his eyes. "She's a royal pain in the ass, but she saved Louis when he was assaulted."

Griff raised an eyebrow. "She found him?"

Quinn smirked. "She sent a waitress after him because she wanted his attention. Without her, Louis would have probably died."

"She can be the biggest pain in the ass ever," Craig declared, "but she's got an open house to every club in the city."

"She can also alibi Jem," Louis said.

Griff looked at Louis who had just joined them. "How's that?"

"When Jem arrived back here, he didn't go straight upstairs. He went through the VIP section in the club, talking to people as he usually does. He spoke to Conchita briefly. Darius for longer. I know him from Romero. He likes to complain. Then Jem spoke to one of the bartenders before he went in search of Max. Jem also went into the kitchen too. He's got a rock-solid alibi from the time you dropped him off until he goes up to the apartment."

"As far as the cops are concerned, he could still have shot Max," Craig pointed out. "He could have shot him, hid the weapon, and then called the cops."

"You're not helping," Quinn said sourly.

Griff folded his arms across his chest and scowled at Craig. "Then we need to help him. Because I'm not leaving him here by himself. He's coming back to my place."

"He won't be allowed to stay here. The apartment is a crime scene. He's have to find somewhere to stay," Quinn said. "There's no gunshot residue on his hands or clothes. I made sure they tested him immediately. And there's no sign of the weapon."

Griff gave Quinn a grateful smile. At least someone had Jem's back. "When Max wakes up he'll be able to confirm Jem is innocent."

"*If* he wakes up," Craig added, giving Griff an apologetic look. "There's a good chance he's not going to."

"Dammit." Griff knew the cops would be looking for a quick arrest. He didn't believe they would necessarily pin it on Jem, but he was the obvious suspect.

"Do we know who Jem's lawyer is?" Louis asked.

Quinn nodded. "Dominic does, and he's handling it."

Griff hated the fact that everybody else seemed to know what was going on and he didn't. He wanted to be able to support Jem but, in reality, he barely knew him.

He looked up as Louis squeezed his shoulder.

"Jem is going to need you," Louis said softly. "We can handle the details, but Jem is going to need somebody to take care of him, and that's you."

Quinn gave Griff a hard stare. "I know you're on vacation, but the situation has changed now. If we accept that Jem is innocent—"

"He *is* innocent," Griff snapped.

"If we accept that Jem is innocent," Quinn repeated, "Then Jem could also be in danger. We have teams set up here, but he will need a personal bodyguard."

"Dominic is okay with that?"

"You're part of my team," Quinn said.

"I wasn't," Griff muttered, but Quinn ignored him.

"If you need to get out of the city, Mo has the spare cabin. But the cops will probably want him to stay close, at least initially, and Jem will want to be close to his brother. He could come and stay with me as Cade is away."

"No." Griff shook his head. Under no circumstances was he allowing Jem to stay with another Daddy.

"I would expect you to come too," Quinn said, like Griff was being stupid.

"I can't leave Doris, and I don't think your cat would appreciate sharing her space with a big slobbery rottie."

Quinn's one-eyed cat was old, cranky, and three times as scary as Doris.

Quinn pulled a face. "You're right there. I hadn't considered that. Take Jem back to your apartment, and we'll put on extra security if we need to."

Louis nudged Griff's arm. "He's finished with the cops."

Griff saw Jem coming toward him, dressed in a paper jumpsuit and booties, his dark hair a far cry from its usual elegant style. His barely controlled grief was visible in the lines of stress etched on his face. He'd aged a decade in the couple of hours since Griff had seen him. Without a word, he strode up to Jem and enfolded him in his arms, making sure his back was to everyone else so they couldn't see Jem crying.

"It's all right," Griff crooned. "I'm here. You're not on your own. You don't have to do this by yourself."

Jem's shoulders shuddered. Then he raised his head, tears rolling down his face. "They think I did it. They think I'm the one who shot my brother."

Chapter Six

Jem

It had taken him a while to realize that the police thought he was the one responsible for shooting Max. The questions had gone on ad nauseam, but they always returned to the same thing. Why was Max in his apartment, and where was the gun? Why had Max said his name over and over? The first time, Jem had just stared at them and asked, "What gun?"

They looked at him as if he were stupid. "The gun that shot your brother."

They stopped short of saying the gun that he'd used on his brother, but Jem had finally grasped that was what they meant. Even when Jem had protested that he'd never used a gun in his life and didn't keep one in the apartment, the questions had circled around to the same thing again. They'd taken his clothes and his shoes and tested his hands for gunshot residue. It had been negative, which seemed to annoy the detective rather than corroborate Jem's story. Jem started to suspect the detective wanted an easy conclusion to the case. Maybe he was being unfair on them, as he was the one who'd found Max. But he was tired and scared, and desperately needing Griff's arms around him. Finally the interview was over, but they'd curtly informed him he couldn't stay in the apartment as it was now a crime scene. He'd have to find somewhere else to stay.

The second Griff spotted him, Jem knew he was not on his own. Griff came at once to his side, wrapping his arms around him, and shamefully Jem let go of the grief he'd been holding back. He didn't move from Griff's arms, needing the tight embrace to keep him grounded. He was in the arms of his Daddy, and Griff would keep him safe.

"I need to go to the hospital to be with Max," he whispered to Griff.

He didn't care that the police thought he was the prime suspect. He loved his brother and he had to be with him.

Griff nodded, and looked over at the detectives who were talking to Quinn. "Can Mr. Peacock go to the hospital?"

It hadn't even occurred to Jem that they would stop him.

Detective Hamilton looked over with a sour expression. "Yes, he can go."

"He needs clothes," Griff told Quinn.

Quinn looked at Hamilton who gave a curt nod.

"You've got two minutes," the detective said.

They both disappeared up the stairs to the apartment. Griff looked down at Jem.

"We'll go to the staff bathroom and you can clean up."

Jem knew he had streaks of blood and whatever the crime scene techs had used on his hands. He felt dirty, as if he were covered in Max's life force.

Griff kept hold of him as he led Jem to the private bathroom. It was small, but it was clean. Griff lifted Jem and placed him on the sink counter, then he peeled down the jumpsuit to Jem's waist and very gently started to clean away the blood smears. Jem looked in the mirror to see his face was covered in blood too.

He sat passively, letting Griff work, too exhausted to put up any protest. Griff told him what he was doing all the time as if Jem needed to know. But the sound of his voice was comforting, and Jem didn't even need to listen to what he was actually saying.

A knock at the door disturbed them, then Quinn poked his head around and held out a small pile of clothes, plus a pair of shoes. Jem was relieved to see there were socks tucked into the shoes.

"I don't know what you've got here. The crime scene guy dug around for these. I'm sorry, Jem."

"It's got to be better than a paper jumpsuit," Jem managed.

Quinn flashed him a quick smile then he was gone.

"Let's get this jumpsuit off you."

Griff knelt and tugged it down Jem's thighs. He pulled it off and the booties at the same time.

Jem thanked God he still had his briefs on. But Griff didn't seem fazed by Jem's nakedness. He helped Jem into a pale grey cashmere sweater and a pair of dress pants, then put him back on the counter to roll on the socks and put on the shoes.

"Whoever picked these had some taste," Jem quipped.

"Just be thankful I didn't choose your clothes," Griff said with a chuckle. "You'd be wearing a T-shirt and jeans."

"I don't own any T-shirts or jeans," Jem pointed out, horrified at the thought.

Griff chuckled again. "That's what I live in. I have a

couple of suits for work, but the rest of the time I live in jeans or leathers."

Jem shuddered at the thought. He had always dressed as if he were ready to go out for the evening. Max laughed at him, but he was comfortable in smart clothes.

Max! He shuddered again as he thought about his brother.

"Hey."

Jem looked up as Griff ran the back of his knuckles gently over Jem's cheek.

"It's all right. Your brother is going to be all right."

"You don't know that. The cop said it was touch and go."

"Let's get to the hospital and find out how he really is," Griff said.

Jem nodded and Griff picked him up off the counter. Before Jem could take a step, Griff gathered him into his arms. Jem leaned against him, again amazed at how comforted he felt in Griff's arms. It had been years since he'd let anyone touch him like this. Griff held him for a moment, then stepped back.

"We're going to go to the hospital, then you're coming back to my place for the rest of the night."

"It's all right. I can find a hotel to stay in."

Griff shook his head. "There's something you need to think about."

Jem furrowed his brow. "What?"

"Your brother was shot in your apartment. What if the shooter thought Max was you?"

Jem stared at him in horror. "Why would someone want to shoot me? It doesn't make sense."

"We have no idea. It's too early to say. But CDR is

taking over your personal security. I'm your bodyguard 24/7 until this matter has been resolved."

"Okay," Jem said slowly. "But why can't I go to a hotel?"

"Because I think you'll be more comfortable with me than living in a hotel. Besides which, you know Doris will be unhappy away from home, and she'll have to come with us. I'm not going to leave her for my neighbor to steal."

Jem gave him a dry look. "You just want to get me into your bed, don't you?"

He cursed himself for saying the words before they were out of his mouth. What was he thinking?

But Griff just smiled and said, "You got me."

Before Jem could get himself into more trouble, there was another knock and Quinn was there again, like a wild-haired jack-in-a-box.

"Good, you're dressed. I've just spoken to the hospital and your brother is still in surgery. He's going to be in there for some hours yet."

"Is he still...?" Jem couldn't bring himself to say the word.

"He is still alive," Quinn confirmed. "I'm not going to lie to you, Jem. Max is very lucky to be alive so far. Griff will drive you to the hospital, with backup from CDR's biker guards, Jace and Padraig."

"I thought they were on assignment," Griff said.

"They were, but the client decided he didn't need us any longer."

Jem caught the look Quinn shot Griff. "You were sacked by the client?"

Quinn shrugged. "It happens. I told the client he was a stupid fool, but there's nothing I can do about it if he insists."

"You can put him over your knee and spank his ass," Griff muttered.

"Mo would kill me if I laid a finger on his boy," Quinn pointed out. "Besides which, I hear the spanking has already happened. But Joseph insists that now Carrington White is decorating the bottom of a ravine, he's safe."

Jem looked between them in horror. "What happened?"

"I'll tell you all about it on the way to the hospital," Griff assured him.

Jem left the bathroom, wondering not for the first time what the hell he'd gotten himself into.

The detective who'd questioned him approached with a grim look on his face. "You need to be at the precinct tomorrow morning at ten."

Jem nodded in agreement, and the detective's expression relaxed a fraction.

"Do I need my lawyer?"

"He's coming with his lawyer," Quinn said before the detective could speak.

The detective's face hardened, but he nodded and stepped away. Griff led Jem through the now empty club, toward the back exit.

"There are press at the front of the building. My car is parked outside the back exit."

"Do you think they're going to arrest me?"

Griff stopped and looked at him. "They're not going to arrest. You didn't do anything. They're just trying to rattle you. You won't be going anywhere without me...one of us and your lawyer."

Griff believed in him. Jem could cope if Griff thought he was innocent. He needed someone to have his back.

Griff opened the back door and lights exploded in Jem's eyes.

Griff

Griff was in front of Jem. He ignored the shouts and the calls for Jem to answer questions, and let Quinn, Mo, and Craig push the paparazzi back so that Griff could guide Jem to his car. This wasn't his first time dealing with the press.

He got Jem into the passenger seat and then rushed around to slide in behind the wheel. The keys were in the ignition, and he gunned the engine. He just hoped the photographers weren't stupid enough to get in front of the car. But the other bodyguards had done their job, and he had a clear run down the alley. As they reached the sidewalk he could see Jace and Padraig waiting for him. They were out and driving toward the intersection before the men waiting on the sidewalk realized who they were.

"Someone let them know we were going to come out of that exit," Jem said with a shaky voice.

Griff had a gut feeling he knew who'd done that. For some reason, the detective had an issue with Jem. He was going to find out what it was.

"Do you think the media will be at the hospital too?"

"I think they'll try," Griff said grimly. "But CDR will handle it."

He wanted to know how the press had gotten down the alley without CDR finding out. This was a conversation he was gonna have as soon as they got to the hospital.

"It's going to be all over the local news, isn't it?"

"I'm afraid so," Griff confirmed. "Do you have a publicity firm who can handle this for you?"

"Yes. Max usually speaks to them, but I can call them."

"No," Griff said. "Call Quinn and get him to handle it. All you need to do is focus on your brother."

"Okay. Okay." Jem sounded unsure but he patted

himself and then groaned. "I left my phone in the apartment."

"Take mine." Griff pulled his out of his pocket, unlocked it, and handed it over to Jem.

"Hi, Quinn, it's Jem. Uh... Griff suggested you could call my publicity company and ask them to handle the media. My phone is in the apartment so I can't give you the number, but the company is Sarah Reynolds PR. We usually deal with Sarah Reynolds herself." Jem was silent for a moment. "It's what we pay them to do. Yes, I'll tell him."

Jem disconnected the call and looked at Griff. "Quinn said the press got an anonymous phone call to tell them we'd be coming out the back exit."

"I'm sure they did," Griff growled.

"I wonder if the PR company will sack us as a client," Jem mused.

Griff snorted. "I've met a few PR companies, and they live for this sort of publicity. If the cops try to pin this on you, you'll be the poster boy for the wrongly accused."

"You've met Sarah, I gather."

"They are a breed," Griff assured him. He was pleased to see Jem give a weak smile.

Griff's phone rang and after a nod from Griff, Jem answered it. "Jem here. Yes, I'll put it on speaker. What have you got for me?"

"Your PR woman is one scary broad," Quinn said. "She all but accused me of letting the press know where we'd be. She's told me to tell you she's already handling it. Your lawyer is in place for the meeting at the precinct tomorrow morning. And there's a statement being released by her about press and police harassment."

Jem chuckled. "I guess she's not going to sack me."

"Her exact words were, 'Thank God I've got something to do now'."

"She's always complaining that she represented the most boring club in the city, because nothing bad ever happened. Now she's going to have to eat her words."

Griff was relieved Jem had professionals on his side. He wasn't surprised, but he had been assigned to clients before who failed to understand the power of harnessing the press.

"Jace and Padraig will ensure you can get to the OR without being bothered. Mo is already there threatening them with legal action if they let a journalist anywhere near you or Max."

"We're supposed to be nice to these people," Griff pointed out.

"My cup of niceness ran out when I discovered cops were making sneaky phone calls."

"You thought it was him too?"

"Yes," Quinn said in the grimmest tone Griff had heard. "And I don't know why he's got a hate boner for you, Jem, but I'm gonna find out."

Then he was gone. Jem sat back with a sigh of relief. "I suppose this is a normal day for you."

Griff snorted. "These are the days our clients pay us to avoid. We like boring days too."

They arrived at the hospital, Griff letting Jace sweep ahead of them, Padraig a silent leather-clad presence at their back. Griff parked as close to the entrance as he could, relieved not to see any press gathering by the door. The three of them surrounded Jem as they all headed into the hospital.

"I know where we're going," Jace said, and headed for the elevators.

Griff was relieved when the elevator doors opened, and

it was empty. They piled in and Jem leaned against him. Griff could see how tired he looked. The adrenaline was crashing now, and Jem was probably forcing himself to keep going. Griff ran his hand up and down Jem's back. "You'll probably be able to get some sleep before you can see Max."

"The last time I was here, I was waiting for news of my parents," Jem said bleakly.

Griff put his arms around Jem. He wanted to tell Jem that it wouldn't be like the last time, but his brother had been shot at point-blank range. If he were lucky, the bullet wouldn't have hit anything vital. But if the shooter knew what they were doing, Max's chances were slim.

At the OR reception, they were pointed to a blandly decorated waiting room.

Griff tugged Jem down next to him on one of the couches. He looked at Jace and Padraig. "Are you going back to the office or home?"

Padraig shook his head. He was an older man, stocky and blunt featured. He was also a demon on the motorbike. If he had been a Daddy, he would have been a Biker Daddy Bodyguard without question. As it was, he was happily married, and didn't care who he guarded as long as they did what they were told. Jace was a handsome black guy, wedded to his job as much as his fiancée. Griff had great respect for them both.

"We're staying with you for the rest of the night. Jace wants to meet Doris."

Griff managed a smile. Doris was notorious for winning the hearts of all the CDR men. Even the gruff old guys like Padraig.

"I'll get coffee for us all," Jace said.

"I'm not drinking anything from a vending machine," Padraig grumbled.

Jace rolled his eyes. "You've been spoiled by working for Joseph."

Padraig shrugged. "He has the best coffee of any of the clients I've worked for."

"Don't tell him that," Jem said. "You know he'll be unbearable."

They all smirked at each other. Mo's boy was the biggest brat on the block, and now Mo had his hands full taming Joseph Holden.

Jace disappeared and Jem knuckled his eyes.

"Don't do that," Griff scolded. "You'll make them sore."

"Too late," Jem murmured, but he immediately put his hands in his lap.

Padraig watched the exchange with a minimal eye roll. He was too used to the Daddies and boys now.

"How long do you think Max will be in surgery?" Jem asked.

"I'll go find out," Padraig said.

Griff was glad of a few minutes to gather Jem against his chest and hold him tight. He brushed the lightest of kisses against Jem's soft hair.

Jem sighed and burrowed into him, unconsciously seeking comfort. "I don't think we'll get our session tomorrow."

"I don't think so either," Griff agreed. "I didn't expect to see you straight after leaving you here at the club."

"Thank you for coming back. I don't know if I could handle this without you." Jem said.

"Of course."

It was a given. There was no way he'd leave Jem to handle this tragedy alone. He was going to be at Jem's side until it was all over, and beyond, if Jem would let him.

They looked up as someone walked in, but it was Jace

with the coffee. He must have read Jem's disappointed face because he said, "Padraig's talking to the nurse now."

It was another five minutes before Padraig returned, but hard on his heels was a tired -looking woman in scrubs.

"Are you here for Mr. Peacock?" she asked.

Jem handed his coffee to Griff and stood. "I'm Max's brother. How is he?"

Chapter Seven

Jem

"He's in recovery. We managed to remove the bullet. Max was very lucky. It nicked his lung, but the surgeon managed to repair the damage."

Jem stared at her for a moment, not quite able to believe what she was saying. "He's going to be all right?"

"He's got a long road ahead of him, but the operation was a success."

Jem noticed she avoided the question. "Can I see him?"

"Soon. We need to run tests and then you can see him."

Jem thought his legs were going to give way, the relief overwhelming. But suddenly Griff's arms were around him, guiding him to sit down on the seat he'd just vacated.

The nurse gave a tired smile then vanished, and Griff held him close.

"It's all right," Griff crooned in his ear.

Jem pressed his face into Griff's shoulder and shuddered, not able to hold back the tears.

"We'll give you a minute," Jace said.

"We'll be right outside the door," Padraig said. "No one will be able to come in."

Jace and Padraig vacated the room, leaving him alone with Griff. Griff's arms were tight and Jem let the tears flow. He knew he was going to have to get it together soon, but he just needed a few minutes to break down. He remembered the time he'd been here with Max, waiting for news of their parents. Then the doctor had come to deliver the bad news. He and Max were orphans. It had been shocking and over-whelming, and there had been no letup from it. No one to tell him everything would be all right. He and Max had clung to each other in desperation.

Jem was fiercely grateful Griff was here, otherwise he would be waiting alone, knowing that the police suspected him of shooting Max. Griff smelled of laundry detergent and Doris. Jem found it comforting. Somewhere out there was a stocky, slobbery dog that adored this man. He could put his trust in Griff because Doris did.

The tears didn't last long. He sat up and wiped his cheeks with the back of his hand. "I'm sorry about that."

Griff pulled out a paper tissue and wiped Jem's eyes and cheeks, then told him to blow, which Jem did. "You don't have to apologize for crying, ever."

Jem snuffled and nodded. "At least we know he's going to be all right. I don't know how he managed to survive being shot at point blank range."

"He's very lucky," Griff said thoughtfully.

Jem narrowed his eyes. "What are you thinking?"

"I need to think about it," Griff said. "Your brother is alive, and that's all we have to worry about tonight. You should be able to see him soon."

Jem sagged against him in relief. He didn't feel any

desire to pull away from Griff's arms. He stayed where he was, listening to Griff's heartbeat as Griff stroked his hair.

The same nurse returned, and Jem sat up hopefully.

"You can see him now briefly," she said. "Just Mr. Peacock," she added as Griff stood with Jem.

Griff opened his mouth to protest, but Jem smiled at him. "It's all right, I won't be long."

"We'll wait outside the door," Griff said firmly. He sounded as if he was prepared to have a fight about it.

But the nurse merely said, "Come on then."

Jem followed her out of the room, and the three men fell into step behind him. The nurse raised an eyebrow, but she said nothing more as she led Jem to a set of double doors. She paused there.

"He's sedated so don't expect any conversation from him. The police have already been here asking if they can interview him."

Jem looked around nervously. "Where are they?"

"I told them to come back in the morning."

Jem breathed a sigh of relief. He wasn't emotionally up to dealing with the cops at this point.

"He's got a lot of machines around him, but just focus on your brother."

In desperation, Jem turned to Griff who squeezed his shoulder.

"I'll be here waiting for you," Griff promised.

Jem gave a curt nod, then followed the nurse into recovery. He could do this for Max.

He was glad the nurse had given him a warning, otherwise he might have freaked out at the number of machines around Max. His big brother looked very small in the hospital bed. He was used to Max laughing and joking and moving. To see him so still just didn't seem right.

"Oh Maxy, who did this to you?" Jem murmured as he took Max's hand in his. "I promise I'll find out and make them pay." He heard a cough behind him and realized the nurse was still in the room. He smiled at her ruefully. "You didn't hear that, did you?"

"Hear what?"

"He'll kill me for calling him Maxy."

"I promise I won't tell him," she said with a smirk.

"How long will he stay here?"

"A few hours. We need to make sure he's stable. I'm going to send you home in a minute."

Jem was about to protest, but she said, "You need to sleep, and your brother is going to be out of it for hours. We've given him pretty heavy sedation. We'll call you if there's any change in his condition."

Jem wondered if this was because the cops had told them he was a suspect.

But the nurse smiled at him kindly. "Let your boyfriend take you home, and you can pretend to sleep."

"He's not my—"

"You tell him that," she said with a laugh.

Jem wasn't going to argue with that. Griff had been very possessive.

He bent down and kissed Max on the forehead, then she escorted him out of the recovery room. Griff, Jace, and Padraig were lined up outside the double doors like wooden soldiers.

The nurse rolled her eyes. "Take him home and make sure he gets some sleep."

Griff wrapped his arm around Jem's shoulders. "Yes, ma'am," he agreed.

"I should stay here in case he needs me," Jem said.

"We'll call you," she promised.

"Take my number," Griff said. "Jem's phone is back at the club."

Griff gave the nurse his phone number and, reluctantly, Jem let Griff lead him away.

"I could stay at the hotel across the street."

Griff shook his head. "No, you're coming back to my apartment. We've already had this discussion. It's okay, I can get you here in under ten minutes. Your brother is in good hands. And all you would be doing is sitting on uncomfortable chairs and drinking bad coffee."

"Quinn has arranged a security detail for your brother," Padraig said. "We're staying with you."

Jem nodded. He wasn't sure about any of this. He suddenly felt out of control of his own life. He was a suspect in his own brother's shooting. He couldn't go back to his home. He couldn't even stay in the hotel because Griff insisted he come back to his apartment. He wondered what would happen if he had a meltdown here and now.

"It's all right," Griff murmured in his ear.

Jem hadn't realized that he'd stopped walking. "Nothing's all right," he said brokenly. "I have no idea what I'm doing."

"Let me do the thinking for you, just for tonight. Tomorrow morning we'll come here and check on your brother before you go to the precinct. But you won't be doing any of it alone. I'll be with you all the way."

"What about the club?"

Financially, he and Max were wealthy, and a few days being closed wouldn't affect them. He could afford to pay the staff too. But that couldn't go on forever.

"We'll talk to the cops tomorrow. The club itself isn't a crime scene so I can't see why they won't let it open, but you probably won't be able to go back to your apartment."

Jem didn't care about that. He wasn't sure he would ever be able to walk back into his apartment again. He didn't say that though. He just let Griff lead him out of the hospital and into his car. It seemed easier to let Griff do what he wanted. He couldn't put a coherent thought together.

He stared out of the window as they travelled the short distance to Griff's apartment. He'd thought he'd be returning here for a session as a boy. Would that ever happen? He hoped so. He needed his Daddy more than ever.

Griff

Griff knew Jem was in shock. He had handled many clients like Jem before. He let Doris love on him in the hallway, then led Jem to his bedroom, putting his bag down by his feet.

"You can sleep in my bed tonight. Padraig and Jace will be in the main room."

Jem looked at him uncertainly. "Where are you going to sleep?"

"I'll be outside the door."

"I can't take your bed."

Griff took Jem's hands in his. "Usually I'd arrange a bed in the playroom for you, but I think you'd prefer it if we stayed out of the playroom tonight."

He wasn't surprised when Jem nodded in agreement. Stepping into that world was something Jem wasn't prepared to do with the other two men there.

"I haven't got another bedroom. Don't worry, you'll be quite safe," Griff assured him.

Jem licked his lips. "Please, Daddy, stay with me."

"Are you sure?" Griff didn't want to pressure Jem into doing anything that he didn't want to, especially as he must be feeling extremely vulnerable.

"I need to know that you are near me."

"Let me talk to the boys and then I'll be back."

At Jem's weary nod, Griff left the bedroom to talk to Padraig and Jace, who were making coffee in the kitchen and discussing plans for the night. Padraig was on the floor with Doris, rubbing her belly. Griff knew he had lost Doris. Usually she slept at the end of his bed, but whenever he had guests, the dog stayed with them. He tried not to feel hurt about it.

"Jem and I are sharing the bedroom. Help yourself to anything you want. The fridge is full. I'm gonna try and get a few hours' sleep before we go back to the hospital."

"Are you expecting trouble? Is there any reason Jem would think someone would be after him?" Padraig asked.

It was a fair question. Griff shook his head. "This is a bolt out of the blue for Jem. Until his brother wakes up, I doubt we're gonna get any further with the case." He yawned and looked at his clock. "Jeez, it's three a.m.. No wonder I'm tired. Call me if you hear anything strange. The neighbor next door gets up at dark thirty to exercise. He can be enthusiastic about it."

Padraig pulled a disgusted face. "Thanks for the warning."

Griff returned to the bedroom to find Jem sitting cross legged on the bed, still fully dressed.

"Jem, it's time to sleep."

Jem didn't move. Griff sat on the bed next to him.

"Let's get you undressed."

He slowly undressed Jem, kneeling at his feet to take off his shoes and socks, then laying the cashmere sweater and dress pants over the chair. Jem let him, not reacting at all.

Griff disappeared into his closet and came back with a T-shirt and sleep shorts. "These should fit you."

Jem stared at the sleepwear and then looked up at Griff. "Dinosaurs?"

"Next time we can discuss the choice of decoration."

It was the first reaction Jem had given him, so Griff didn't mind too much.

Griff helped him on with the T-shirt and shorts. "You want to use the bathroom?" At Jem's nod, he said "There are fresh toothbrushes under the sink. Help yourself."

Jem disappeared into the bathroom and Griff took the opportunity to get undressed for bed. He usually slept naked, but today he dressed the same as Jem, with dinosaurs.

Jem's lips twitched when he saw what Griff was wearing. Griff grinned at him and then disappeared into the bathroom himself.

He returned to find Jem standing where he'd left him. "Is everything all right?"

"I wasn't sure which side of the bed to go on," Jem confessed.

Griff led him to the left-hand side of the bed and pulled back the covers. Jem slipped in and Griff covered him up.

"Are you all right with the light turned out?" Griff asked.

"I'm fine." Jem sounded a little surprised at the question, but Griff had worked with some clients who couldn't bear to have the light off. Quinn's boy had a fear of the dark after being abused.

Griff flicked the light off then settled into the bed next

to Jem, careful not to touch him. He was tired and settled down with a sigh of relief. It had been a long day.

"Why do you think my brother was shot?" Jem asked into the silence.

"I've got no idea," Griff said honestly. "But there's always a reason and we'll find out what it is."

"Do you think I did it?"

Griff rolled over to face Jem, although he was little more than a darker shadow in a dark room. "No, I don't think you're responsible for shooting your brother."

"You don't know that. You don't know me."

"You're right. I don't know you, but I believe you when you say you didn't do it."

"But why do you believe me?"

He could tell by the strain in Jem's voice that the answer was very important to him. Griff thought for a moment about what to say. "It's a matter of trust. You're clients of CDR. Dominic, Quinn, and Craig trust you and Max as clients, and I've seen them fire clients before."

"You have?" Jem sounded dubious.

"I've worked for CDR for a long time, and believe me, they don't keep clients who lose their trust."

"So you believe me because CDR trust me?"

"That goes a long way, but there's more to it than that. You could have left me to walk through the club and talk to people, make nice with Conchita, then gone upstairs and shot your brother."

"I could," Jem agreed, his voice hoarse.

"But you didn't."

"How do you know that?"

"Your timing was very narrow. You have no blood splatter on you. The only blood is where you tried to stem the bleeding. You have no gunpowder residue on you. You don't own a gun. We can find no records of you even shooting a gun. There are no weapons in the apartment or in the surrounding area. The police have checked, and you wouldn't have had time to get rid of it."

"That's all circumstantial."

"Yes, but it's building up a picture. You have no motive for killing your brother. Your financial records show that you're both wealthy and free of debt. There are no inheritance issues. It would hardly be love because you're gay and he's...whatever he is. There are no spouses to cause problems."

Jem huffed loudly. "Okay, okay, I get the picture. As far as CDR are concerned, I'm not a likely suspect. But the cops still think it's me."

"The police are going to look for the easiest option. And that's you. You can't blame them, because nine times out of ten it is family. But the difference this time is that you have no motive and very little opportunity. CDR will convince the cops otherwise. You haven't seen Dominic in action."

"You're saying I should go to sleep and stop worrying."

"I'm saying you should focus on your brother. Let me and CDR handle the rest."

Griff didn't know how to convince Jem that he was in the safest of hands. He wouldn't let anything happen to him.

"I'm scared, Daddy."

He barely heard Jem's whispered confession, but it was loud enough that Griff knew he had to reassure his boy.

"Come here, boy," he ordered.

Jem rolled into his arms with a sigh. Griff berated himself for not realizing sooner that was what Jem needed. Jem fitted into his arms like he was made to be there. Griff kissed his soft hair and whispered that he was safe. Jem didn't reply but he relaxed, his hand over Griff's heart, and his breathing slow and steady.

"If you need me to help you, just ask," Griff whispered.

"I will," Jem murmured, his breath warm against Griff's neck.

"I'm your Daddy."

Jem stiffened for a moment but then he relaxed again. "Don't make promises you can't keep."

Griff was momentarily hurt by Jem's comment but he knew that Jem was only protecting himself. "I can keep this promise, but for now accept the help from me as a Biker Daddy Bodyguard. I will protect you; I'll keep you safe from danger, and I will be your Daddy in every instance you need it. Can you believe that?"

Jem was quiet for a long moment, and Griff was worried he'd pushed Jem too far, but then Jem nodded.

"I can believe that. Thank you, Griff... Thank you, Daddy."

Griff hugged him closer. Jem's breathing slowed and he fell into sleep. Griff heard the rumbling voices of Jace and Padraig in the other room, and tumbled soon after into the velvety darkness, reassured by both the conversation and the presence of the other two bodyguards.

Chapter Eight

Jem

Jem wasn't sure where he was. The bed was too hard, the comforter not what he expected to feel, and he could hear voices in another room. As he lived alone, that was kind of worrying.

Then it all came rushing back. Max. Griff. Max was lying in hospital while Jem had slept in Griff's bed. Jem sat bolt upright and looked at the space next to him. It was empty.

He felt a crushing disappointment, and then realized that Griff might be one of the voices he heard in the next room. He needed to get out of bed and find out what was going on. He needed to call the hospital.

The door opened and Griff walked in, smiling when he saw Jem sitting up in bed.

"You're awake. That's good." Griff sounded like he was praising him merely for the act of waking up.

Jem gave him a wan smile. "I need to find out how Max is. I should call the hospital."

"No need. I've already called them. Max is fine. He woke up once during the night, but he was distressed, so they sedated him again."

Crushing guilt overwhelmed Jem. He should have been with his brother, not sleeping with Griff. He pushed back the covers and got to his feet. "I should go and see him."

"You've got time for a coffee and breakfast. Then we're going to see Max before we go to the precinct."

Jem grimaced. He'd forgotten about the appointment with the police officers. He pushed back his hair, wincing as a nail got caught in the strands. "What time is it?"

Griff helped him disentangle his fingers. "It's just after six. I got up early to give Doris a quick walk."

Jem gaped at him. "Just after six? We had about three hours sleep?" No wonder he felt so rough.

"Yeah," Griff said. "I'm sorry for the early start, but I thought you'd want to spend some time with your brother before going to the cops."

Jem pressed his lips together, feeling tears prickling his eyes. It was nice of Griff to be so thoughtful.

"There's coffee ready for you, and I'll make breakfast for everyone. Jace and Padraig are still here."

"I don't think I need anything to eat." Jem wasn't normally awake at six in the morning, let alone functioning.

"You're going to eat breakfast," Griff said firmly. "It's going to be a long day, and I'm not sure when we'll get a chance to eat again."

"I'm not hungry," Jem insisted.

Griff folded his arms across his chest and stared at him. "Boy, you'll do as you are told. You need coffee and something to eat."

Jem glowered back, but finally he looked away, knowing this was one battle he wasn't going to win. Griff could put the food in front of him. It didn't mean to say he was going to eat anything.

"Do I have time for a shower first?"

Griff's expression softened. "Yes, you do. Get in the shower, and I'll bring you coffee to drink."

"In the shower?" Drinking coffee in the shower? That was just plain weird.

Griff snorted and left the bedroom. Jem stared after him then shrugged his shoulders. The whole day was going to be weird. Why was one coffee going to make any difference?

The bathroom was small, and the shower stall about a tenth of the size of his one at home, but the water spray was powerful, and welcome as a wake-up call. He looked at Griff's collection of bottles and blinked. There was a selection of dinosaurs. He picked up a purple stegosaurus. Then he spotted a bottle with a princess in a yellow dress on the front. She looked kind of pretty. He sniffed the contents. Strawberry. Jem smiled happily and squeezed a dollop of that one into his palm and washed himself. He could return to his expensive toiletries tomorrow. There was another dinosaur which contained shampoo, but he ignored that. He wasn't putting cheap shampoo in his hair.

He heard a knock on the door, and Griff said, "May I come in?"

Jem thought about it and then said, his voice somewhat squeaky, "Yes, you can."

In for a penny, in for a pound. Griff had undressed him the night before. There was no point being coy about it.

Griff opened the door of the bathroom, a smile on his face. He held the largest cup Jem had seen, and a towel. He placed the towel on a rail, then walked over to the shower, opened the door slightly, and handed the cup to Jem. "You've got about ten minutes before breakfast is ready."

"Thank you." Jem nearly dropped the cup as his fingers were slippery, but he managed to retrieve the situation with a minimal loss of dignity.

Griff didn't seem to notice. He smiled again and then left Jem to finish his shower. Jem sipped at the coffee and smiled with relief. It was perfect. Just how he liked it. He didn't have long though, and he drank the coffee as quickly as he could, feeling the caffeine burn through him.

Back in the bedroom, he discovered Doris waiting for him. He knelt to give her love and she rumbled happily. Then he rose and looked at the clothes Griff had laid out for him on the bed. They must have been in the bag that had been packed for him. Again they weren't his choice but beggars couldn't be choosers. Jem stared at the briefs left on the bed. They weren't his. He didn't own anything like this. Dark blue with cars over them. These were more like little boy briefs, and he felt disappointed. For a moment he thought about leaving them where they were and looking for his own, but he didn't want to anger Griff. Jem slid them on wishing that Griff was the one dressing him. He dressed in the soft cranberry sweater and dark pants.

He hesitated before he left the bedroom. He knew it was ridiculous. Padraig and Jace had been perfectly friendly to him last night. Jem took a deep breath. He could do this.

The conversation died as he entered the kitchen, and he had a strange feeling they'd been talking about him. But Griff smiled as if he was pleased to see Jem, and Jace and Padraig murmured good morning to him. They both looked exhausted, and Jem felt momentarily guilty, knowing he'd been asleep while they'd been awake all night.

Jace smiled at Jem, reached into his pocket and then held out Jem's cell phone. Someone had cleaned Max's blood off it. "Quinn delivered this an hour ago. Louis is very sorry. He picked up your phone but forgot to hand it over. He couldn't get the charger."

Jem sighed in relief at having his phone back. He could buy a new charger if necessary.

They sat down together at the table. Griff delivered a large stack of pancakes, plus bacon, and said, "There's more if you want it."

Jem looked at it in horror. He never ate in the morning, and pancakes were not his thing, but Jace and Padraig sat down with moans of pleasure. Jem figured that he could leave the three men to eat most of the pancakes, while he nibbled on the fruit. Griff had already left a bowl of chopped up fruit on the table.

Griff came over to the table and served Jem with two pancakes and bacon, and a small bowl of fruit. Jem flushed, but the other two men didn't pay any attention. They laughed and chatted, although it was mainly shoptalk. Jem didn't really listen; his whole focus was on thinking about his brother.

"You need to eat," Griff said, nudging him gently.

Jem stared down at the plate and realized he hadn't eaten a bite. He really wasn't hungry.

"Eat," Griff ordered.

Jem felt his cheeks heat as the conversation died at the table. He glanced up to see Griff staring at him. This was a battle he was going to lose. Jem cut off a bite of pancake and put it in his mouth. It tasted like ashes, but he forced himself to swallow. Then he took another bite. A few minutes later he stared down at his plate. It was empty. He'd eaten everything, including the fruit.

"I was hungrier than I expected," he said in surprise.

"I'm always hungry at this time of day," Jace said. "Especially if I'm doing the night shift."

"You just like other people doing the cooking," Padraig said.

"The Daddy Bodyguards are nearly as good as my fiancée," Jace agreed. "Not that I'd tell her that."

Jem couldn't believe Jace was so laid-back about the Daddies. He looked up to see Griff staring at him. Griff dropped him a wink. This was another world to him, and he was going to have to get used to it.

He helped Griff clear away the breakfast things while Jace and Padraig checked in with CDR. He put the last plate in the dishwasher and straightened to find Griff standing behind him.

Griff smiled down at him. "Thank you for your help, my boy."

Jem glowed under his praise.

"And well done for eating your breakfast."

Jem leaned into his touch. Just the feel of Griff's hands on him grounded him. "I needed the food. Thank you for taking care of me."

"Always," Griff promised, his eyes warm on Jem's. He hugged Jem briefly.

Jem wanted to stay in Griff's arms for the rest of the day. But they had to go if they were going to spend any time with Max. Jem knelt to hug Doris, chuckling as she snuffled in his ear and licked his cheek.

Then they were in the car, traveling back to the hospital, and all the food that Jem had eaten lay heavy in the pit of his stomach.

"It'll be all right," Griff said.

"You don't know that."

"No, I don't, but I'm here. Never forget I'm here."

Griff placed his hand on Jem's knee and Jem tangled their fingers together. He needed the comfort, and was more than willing to accept Griff's.

Griff

Griff took one look at Max and was deeply glad he was with Jem. Max was as white as the sheet he was lying on. Even his lips barely had any color. Jem made a sound, and Griff realized he was choking back a sob.

"Go sit next to him," Griff suggested, "and talk to him."

Jem stayed where he was, and Griff realized that he was frozen. Griff put his arm around Jem and steered him to the side of the bed with the least machines. He put a chair behind Jem and eased him down. Jem didn't react until Griff took his hand and placed it over Max's. Then he started sobbing.

Although it was hard for him, Griff stepped back. Every instinct screamed at him to wrap his arms around the boy, but Jem needed to spend time with his brother.

He stayed near the door, ready to intercept anyone who came into the room. A nurse in blue scrubs popped her head around the door, but when she saw Jem she backed out, mouthing to Griff that she'd come back later. He nodded and gave her a grateful smile.

They had about an hour before they needed to leave for the precinct. Griff was determined to let Jem spend every minute of that with his brother.

The urgency of that became apparent when he received a message from Quinn.

Cops determined to arrest Jem. Don't go without lawyer.

Griff grimaced. This was news he did not want to break

to Jem. He typed a query back and received a swift response.

Cops have something but they're not sharing it with CDR.

He didn't do it.

Griff received an eyeball emoji. Good, Quinn wouldn't have been so laid-back if he thought for a minute that Jem had shot his brother. Jem wasn't the first client to have been suspected of murder, but he was the first for the Biker Daddy Bodyguards. It would be interesting to see how they all reacted when one of their own was involved.

"What's wrong?" Jem said.

Griff looked up from the screen.

"I've been watching you. You got some news you didn't like. What is it?"

Jem must have eyes in the back of his head.

"The cops want to pin this on you." Griff had been going to put it more delicately, but in the end he had to be honest. "Is your lawyer going to be there?"

Jem pulled out his phone and showed the screen to Griff.

See you there 10 o'clock. Uncle D

"Is that your lawyer?"

"Yes. He's a piranha. I don't hold out much hope of the cops managing to pin this on me." Jem sounded remarkably calm for somebody facing a murder rap.

Griff narrowed his eyes. "Quinn thinks they've got something on you, but they're not sharing it with CDR."

He saw Jem shudder. Maybe he wasn't as calm as he was making out.

"I don't know what it could be. I've told you everything."

Griff wasn't sure he believed that, but he had to take it

on face value. They hadn't found anything that would link Jem to his brother's shooting. The fact that the police had found something and weren't sharing was worrying. What also concerned Griff was that he wouldn't be allowed to be with Jem in the interview. He had to put his trust in Jem's lawyer, and Griff never trusted lawyers.

"Would you come over here and hug me?" Jem asked, his voice very small.

Griff was over there in the second, pulling up another chair, and wrapping his arms around Jem so that Jem's head rested against his chest. Jem's hand went up over Griff's heart, which seemed to be his favorite place to rest.

"I'm scared, Daddy," Jem admitted.

"I'm scared too, boy," Griff confessed, needing Jem to know just how much he meant to him.

"What if they do arrest me?"

"Your lawyer will do everything he can to get you out on bail, but it might not be possible."

"You don't have to sugarcoat it for me," Jem said dryly.

Griff huffed, his breath wafting across Jem's hair. "I'm sorry. I'm used to talking to my co-workers. We don't tend to soften anything."

"Uncle Daniel is good, and he'll find a way to get me out if he can."

"Uncle Daniel?" Griff had noticed the Uncle D in the message but not paid much attention to it.

Jem sat up and looked at Max. "He really is my uncle. He's my father's brother."

Griff snapped his fingers. "Daniel Peacock. I didn't realize, I should have."

"You've met my uncle?" Jem looked confused. "I didn't know that."

"He was...a client."

Now Jem's stare turned icy. "A client?"

If there was anything close, Griff would have knocked his forehead against it. Could he have made it sound any more sordid?

"I was on the protection detail for Daniel when he was getting threats against his life. I was just one of several body-guards. There wasn't anything else to it."

Jem didn't look like he believed Griff, but he was telling the truth. "When was this?"

Griff had to think about it. "About five years ago, I think. I got pulled off my regular detail because they needed extra men. It didn't last long because they caught the guy making the threats. Now I realize your uncle looks like you."

Jem relaxed. "We all look like my grandfather. My mother used to joke that she had nothing to do with the family other than being the incubator. It was all Peacock genes."

"You have gorgeous genes," Griff assured him.

Jem blushed beautifully. "I think you might be biased."

"I definitely am," Griff agreed.

"I really needed the session we were going to have today." Jem looked shame-faced. "And I feel guilty for thinking of myself when my brother could be dying."

"We'll get the session together, I promise, my boy. And your brother is still alive. Focus on that."

There was a loud knock at the door, and then Jace came in with a takeout cup in either hand.

"I thought you'd need these before we go," he said.

Griff smiled at his co-worker. "Thanks, man."

"You're welcome. How is your boy doing?"

Griff frowned; why was Jace asking after his boy? But then he realized Jace meant Max. "He's not talking much."

Jem gave a cross between a laugh and a snort. "It makes a change. Usually I can never get him to shut up."

They all exchanged a grin, then Jace left them alone with, "You've got twenty minutes before we need to leave."

Jem turned back to his brother and held his hand. Griff left him to it, as he worried what information the cops would have that could indict Jem.

Even at ten in the morning the precinct was busy. Griff was relieved to see Quinn and Craig talking to Daniel Peacock in the reception area. He looked at Jem, expecting to see him worried or nervous, but it was as if Jem had pulled all the stops out, and he looked professional and relaxed.

"Jem, my boy," Daniel boomed as they crossed the floor to them.

Griff held back the '*my* boy' burning on his tongue and watched as Daniel enfolded Jem in his arms. The resemblance between them was even more obvious now they were side-by-side. And Griff knew instantly what Jem would look like in thirty years. Still handsome, with silver grey hair. He would be a beautiful, sleek, silver fox.

Daniel looked at Griff speculatively. "I know you."

Griff inclined his head. "I was in your protection detail."

"So you were."

Jem raised his head and looked at his uncle. "You never told me you were receiving death threats."

"No," Daniel murmured.

Griff held back a grin. Typical lawyer.

Jem growled at his uncle, but it was water off a duck's back. Then he sobered. "Let's get this over and done with. I don't think I can take much more waiting."

Daniel nodded. "You need to say goodbye to Griff and the others here. They won't be allowed to come with us."

Griff was surrounded by Quinn and Craig, Jace and Padraig. They took up a lot of space, and people had been giving them careful looks. He noticed a couple of cops glowering at them and wondered what that was about. He would ask Quinn later.

Jem bit his lip and then turned to Griff. "See you later."

"I'm not going anywhere," Griff promised. "I'll be here when you come out."

"You should go spend time with Doris."

"We'll do that together."

Griff was determined that he and Jem were going to spend the rest of their lives loving Doris.

A grim-faced cop approached them. "Jeremy Peacock?"

Jem nodded. "That's me."

"Follow me."

Jem threw Griff one last look and then he was gone, the doors closing behind him.

A hand landed on Griff's shoulder. "It'll be all right," Quinn promised.

Griff nodded, but it wouldn't be all right until Jem was back in his arms again.

Chapter Nine

Jem

This time Detective Hamilton had a female partner. She introduced herself as Mitchell and seemed to wear a permanent sneer on her face. But like Hamilton's partner did the previous night, she let the lead detective do most of the talking.

If it hadn't been for his uncle by his side, Jem knew he would have fallen to pieces under the weight of the detectives' questions. He desperately wanted Griff with him, but he knew that was impossible. Detective Hamilton repeated the same questions as they had last night, over and over, and Jem was sure he gave the same answers, but every change in wording was picked over as though he were lying to them.

Finally Uncle Daniel intervened. "My client has answered your questions. Either charge him or let him go."

Detective Hamilton gave Daniel a cool look. "Just one more question, Mr. Peacock."

Jem tensed, because from the way the cop's body

language changed, he could tell this was a gotcha question. "Yes?"

"You say you've never purchased a gun, but records tell us differently."

Hamilton pushed over a form. Jem could see it was from one of the local gun stores. There was a purchase for a Glock 22.

"Take a look at the name on the invoice," the detective almost purred. "Ballistics confirm that this was the weapon used to shoot your brother."

Jeremy Peacock. Jem's blood ran cold. Someone was trying to frame him. But why?

Daniel studied the form carefully. "Jem, is that your signature?"

Jem forced himself to look at the bottom of the form. "That's...that's not my signature." The relief washed over him in a tidal wave. That wasn't anything like his signature.

Hamilton scowled at him. "This is your name and address?"

"Yes, it is, but that's not my signature. Look, I'll show you, if you give me a pen and paper."

When Hamilton didn't make any effort to hand over either, Daniel pushed over his pad and handed him a pen. Jem signed his signature as usual and turned the pad to show the cop.

"It's nothing like the one on the form. I can show you my signature on my driver's license matches this one."

He went to retrieve his wallet with his driver's license, but the cops stopped him with a sharp, "Stay where you are."

Jem stared at them, wide-eyed. "I was just getting my wallet."

He'd been checked over before he went in, so he wasn't

sure why they thought he'd be armed, but he appreciated their concern.

"Okay, get your wallet out, but slowly."

Jem did as he was told, placing the wallet on the table and pushing it over to the cops. His driver's license was visible as soon as Mitchell flipped it open. His signature was clearly the same as the one on the pad, rather than the one on the form.

"You could have faked your signature," Mitchell sneered.

"He could have," Daniel agreed. "Or he could have used a fake name entirely, which would have been more sensible than trying to frame himself, don't you think?" He sounded disgusted with the cops and Jem was more than relieved his uncle was on his side.

Hamilton sat back with a grunt. "You can go, Mr. Peacock. Stay where we can find you."

"If you wish to talk to my client, you can call me," Daniel said coolly. He gave Jem a nod. "Let's go."

Jem allowed Daniel to lead him out of the small interview room and back into the lobby. He dragged in a breath, feeling like he could breathe for the first time in hours. He wasn't sure how long they had questioned him, but it had felt like an eternity.

"Jem."

He turned to find Griff rushing over to him, and he reached out, not caring where he was. Then Griff's arms were around him, holding onto him so tightly it was almost painful, but he didn't care. He didn't want his Daddy to ever let go of him again.

"Did they charge you?" Quinn asked.

Daniel shook his head. "They didn't, and their gotcha was a form from a gun store with Jem's name and address.

We've established that it's a fake signature." He pursed his lips. "They seem very keen to pin this on you, Jem, my boy. I think that you're going to have to keep convincing them that you're innocent."

"Or find the perp ourselves," Griff growled.

"Your job is to keep Jem safe," Quinn ordered. "CDR will continue with their investigations and liaise with Mr. Peacock." He nodded at Daniel.

"I'll leave it in your hands," Daniel said. "Excuse me, Jem, gentlemen. I have a meeting and I have to get back to the office."

Jem watched him stride away as he rested his head on Griff's shoulder.

"I really hope your uncle is a good guy," Craig muttered under his breath.

Jem raised his head. "Why would you say that?"

Quinn rolled his eyes at Craig. "Because the uncle in our last case turned out to be a murdering psychopath."

Griff chuckled although he didn't sound amused. "You know, you're just asking for trouble by saying that."

"Uncle Daniel is not a murdering psychopath," Jem insisted. It was one of the few things he was absolutely sure about. He may have been a piranha in the courtroom, but he was never a murderer.

"Let's go home," Griff suggested.

"I need to see my brother," Jem said. "Is he all right?"

Quinn nodded. "I called the hospital an hour ago. He was fine. He was awake and asking for you, but the nurse explained you were helping the cops with their inquiries."

"Does he know who shot him?" Jem said.

"Let's go and talk to him." Griff gently guided Jem out of the precinct and into the fresh air.

Jem shuddered and pushed closer to Griff. "I didn't know if I was going to see daylight again."

"I was worried too," Griff admitted. "I don't know why they've got their panties in a wad about you."

"Nice," Jem said dryly. "Thanks for that."

"You're welcome, boy."

They split up on the sidewalk outside the precinct. Quinn said he and Craig needed to get back to CDR to talk to Dominic. Griff and Jem headed toward Griff's vehicle, to travel to the hospital.

Jem was confused when Griff suddenly backtracked along the sidewalk. "Where are we going?"

"You need something to eat and drink first. It's been a long time since breakfast."

Not this again. Jem frowned at Griff. He was perfectly capable of going a few hours without food and drink.

"I'm not hungry. I want to see my brother."

Then he saw Griff's expression change. As if Griff suddenly went into full Daddy mode. All of Jem's senses went on high alert.

"You will do as I say, boy. You need food."

Jem opened his mouth to argue, but Griff ignored him and guided him into a coffee shop. He found himself seated at a table, and a panini and a cappuccino were put in front of him.

Griff sat down with the same thing. He picked it up and then noticed Jem wasn't moving. "Eat," he ordered.

Jem stared at the panini as if it were going to move by itself. Then Griff wrapped his larger hand around Jem's.

"Believe me, boy, you will feel better. You've been running on full adrenaline all day. You need to refuel."

"I'm not going to get out of here without eating and drinking, am I?" Jem asked ruefully.

Griff shook his head. "There are times you have to listen to me, and this is one of them."

"I'm not used to someone trying to make decisions about when I eat or drink."

"Well you'd better get used to it because this is how I operate." Griff sounded far too cheerful for his own good.

"You love with food?" Jem's eyes widened as he suddenly realized what he'd said, but Griff didn't seem fazed.

He patted Jem's cheek. "Yes, I love with food. I love other ways too," he assured Jem.

Cheeks heating wildly, Jem picked up his cup. He was sure Griff had been about to say he loved with his dick but had decided against it. Jem really hoped that was what he'd been about to say. He really needed Griff in all ways. He sipped at the cappuccino, feeling the warmth burn through him. His Daddy had made sure he was all right. Jem couldn't quite believe how lucky he was.

Griff

Max Peacock was like a different man from the ashen guy in the bed this morning. He was awake and very vocal as they approached his room. Griff could hear him from down the hall demanding to be discharged so that he could rescue his brother. Jem just sighed.

"He's a bit protective," he explained. Griff hoped Max wasn't too protective or he could foresee battles ahead as they both tried to look after Jem.

Jem opened the door of his brother's room. The nurse who was trying to calm Max looked over her shoulder and her frustrated expression changed as she spotted Jem.

"Good luck," she muttered to Griff as they passed.

Then she fled as though the hounds of hell were snapping at her heels.

"About time," Max snapped.

"It was so nice and peaceful when you were knocked out," Jem mused. "Could we get them to give you more sedation?"

"Fuck you," Max scowled. Then he smiled. "They didn't arrest you then."

"They probably would have if Uncle Daniel hadn't been there," Jem admitted as he rushed over to Max's side. "Thank God you're all right."

"All right might be a bit optimistic," Max admitted, then yelped. "Careful."

Jem hugged him more gently, but he wouldn't let him go.

Griff hung back, letting the two brothers reconnect. The love and connection between them was obvious, despite the bickering. Jem sat down in the chair by the side of the bed and Max looked over at Griff.

"Thanks for taking care of Jem."

"I hope to do more of it."

Okay, opening salvo shot by both of them. Jem rolled his eyes. "Down boys. We can worry about a pissing contest later. What the hell happened, Max?"

Max shook his head. "I have no idea. All I remember is walking out to the back of the club and then I woke up here."

"So you didn't see who shot you?" Griff queried.

"And you weren't in the apartment?" Jem added, confused now, as the police had been insistent the apartment had been the scene of the crime.

"I can remember a figure, big, definitely a man. He was dressed in black which is why I couldn't really see him at first. I asked him what he was doing there, and then that's the last thing I remember. The nurse said I might have hit my head as I fell. I don't have a concussion so I might remember what happened at some point."

"The police could still think it was me," Jem said, feeling sick at the thought.

But Max shook his head again. "No. I would recognize you anywhere. The man was taller and bigger. He was built more like the huge guy from CDR." He looked at Griff.

"Quinn Ryder," Griff supplied.

"Yeah, him. He could have made two of you," Max added to his brother.

Jem furrowed his brow. "Why did you keep saying my name when I found you?"

"I wanted you to get the hell out of there," Max said. "I didn't know if the guy had gone. But you kept interrupting."

Griff breathed a sigh of relief. No matter what the police said, it was becoming very evident that Jem could not be the perpetrator. That still left a lot of questions.

"Why didn't the shooter show up on the CCTV then?" Jem said, before Griff could ask any more questions.

"If he knew where the cameras were, he could make sure his face wasn't spotted," Griff said. "You said the hallway was dark. Are the lights usually off?"

Max furrowed his brow. "You know, you're right. We usually keep all the lights on, and that's the reason I investigated. I thought a client must have gone down there by mistake and switched the lights off on their return."

"Somebody knew where the cameras were, knew the routine enough to turn off the lights." Griff chewed on his bottom lip. "We still don't know if you were the target. You are of a similar height and build. You look alike. And in the dark the shooter could have mistaken you for Jem."

"But why would anyone want to attack Jem?" Max scoffed. "He's harmless."

"Thanks," Jem said dryly.

Griff grinned as he remembered a conversation with Mo about his boy's fury at being called harmless in a CDR report. "So far we've had a manic fan, an abusive Daddy, a driver, a club employee, and a family member attack the boys in our care."

Now it was Max's turn to furrow his brow. "I thought there'd been three cases?"

"Three of them were Cade Connolly's. He always was an overachiever," Jem said.

"Still, the point remains," Griff said. "We don't know which one of you they were targeting or why, come to that."

Max laid back against the pillows, suddenly looking exhausted. No matter how much he complained, he wouldn't be going anywhere tonight. "I assume the cops are gonna come and talk to me at some point."

"It can wait until tomorrow," Griff said. "You need to sleep."

"I'm fine," Max insisted. Then he yawned which completely belied his protest. "Maybe I'll just have a nap."

Jem bent over and kissed his forehead. "I'll come back in the morning. You need to rest."

"Where are you staying?" Max asked sleepily.

"He staying with me," Griff said.

Max opened one eye. "Good, you take care of him."

"I will," Griff promised.

Jem stayed where he was a moment until Max's heavy breathing turned into light snoring. They left the room and headed toward the nurses' station.

The nurse that had run from the room looked up as they approached. "Don't tell me, he's asleep."

"Snoring like a baby," Jem said with a grin.

"I knew he'd wear himself out eventually," the nurse said. "They always shout and holler to get out of bed, and then they crash out to sleep."

"We'll be back in the morning, unless you think we should stay?" Griff asked.

"He'll sleep most of the night. He's still on heavy pain relief. We'll ease it off tomorrow and he should be more alert. You both look exhausted. Go home and get some rest."

Jem looked torn between his desire to be with his brother and his obvious need to sleep. Griff decided not to give him any choice. He wrapped an arm around Jem's shoulders, wished the nurse a good night, and led him to the elevators.

Jem gave a huge sigh and leaned against Griff as they waited for the elevator. "You're coming back to my place," Griff said, before Jem could start worrying about it.

"I don't think I can face the club or being on my own," Jem admitted. "It's been a long day."

"And we had very little sleep last night. We're going to go home, give Doris an evening walk, and go to bed. At least you know your brother is all right."

"Now he's awake and yelling like he normally does, I feel a lot better."

"At least he can tell the cops it wasn't you." At Jem's silence, Griff turned to see his pensive expression. "Jem?"

"He can tell them, but will they listen?" Jem asked. "You didn't hear them. It was like they wanted to blame me, no matter what the evidence said. I've never felt so helpless."

"Detective Hamilton certainly seems to have an agenda. Have you met him before?"

Jem shook his head. "I've been racking my brains to

think why I might have annoyed him, but I'm sure I've never met him. I don't even remember him being a member of the club."

"I'll get Quinn to look into it." Griff didn't want Jem having to fight fires on two fronts. It was bad enough they didn't know who had shot Max, but being in the cops' crosshairs, even in the face of evidence to the contrary, would ramp up the anxiety.

"Poor Doris," Jem said suddenly. "She's been on her own all day."

"She's been living it up with my neighbor. Poor Doris has had walks and treats and scratches all day. She's fine."

"Perhaps your neighbor would give me walks and treats and scratches," Jem teased.

"I don't think so," Griff growled.

The doors opened to the elevator. They stepped in and Griff was relieved to see it was empty. He tugged Jem into his arms and held him close, relieved when Jem relaxed against him.

Suddenly, Jem shot up so fast he nearly smacked Griff in the chin. It was only Griff's reflexes that saved them both from harm.

"What's the matter?"

"I just remembered something. Max had a visitor last week. I was out, and I came back to find Max showing someone out. I asked him who it was, because he looked annoyed, but he just said it was something to do with the business. I was surprised at the time, because usually he shares business discussions with me. He all but told me to keep my nose out of it. I would have pursued it, but I was...distracted."

The color on his cheeks told Griff exactly what he was distracted with.

"I'll pass this on to Quinn. If the visitor came to the club, CDR should have a record of it."

Jem's expression darkened. "I should have told you before, but Max has a habit of bypassing security when he brings men into the club."

Griff stared at Jem, a sinking feeling in the pit of his stomach. "You're joking?"

"I wish I were, but he's done it for years."

"That means there's a good chance we won't be able to find out who did this."

"I know," Jem said miserably.

Chapter Ten

Jem

Jem could feel Griff seething all the way back to his apartment. It hadn't occurred to him to mention it before, because they were looking for the shooter, not a man his brother had picked up for the night. Max had always insisted the security was for the club, not his private life. And he wasn't going to change the way he operated just because the security firm said so.

But now it looked as if Max's careless behavior had finally let him down. Max would be furious with Jem for confiding in Griff, but Jem couldn't feel sorry about that. Not if it led them to catching the shooter. As Griff parked the car in the underground parking lot, he looked over at Jem.

"I'm not angry with you, boy. It's been a very traumatic forty-eight hours, and I'm not surprised you've only just remembered these details. I need to call Quinn to let him know and then we can relax. Now Max is awake, Quinn and the cops can get all the information from him. We just need to focus on you."

Jem nodded miserably. "I should have remembered sooner. The cops were questioning me on Max's private life."

Griff patted his knee. "It's okay, Jem. Max will have to change the way he operates, but he's alive. We'll find out who tried to hurt him, I promise you."

Jem was reassured but he still wished he'd remembered it sooner. He let Griff lead him back to the apartment and knelt to accept Doris's slobbery kisses in greeting.

"I see Doris is sharing her affections."

Jem looked over his shoulder to see a tall, handsome man in his forties giving him a rueful smile. This must be the next-door neighbor. Jem tried not to glare at him.

"You know she's a tart," Griff said, grinning at Rob.

"I do." Rob narrowed his eyes as he contemplated Jem. "I know you. Why do I know you?"

"Rob, this is Jem Peacock. Jem, this is my irritating next-door neighbor who my dog loves far too much."

Rob laughed at Griff's less than complimentary introduction. "It's not my fault you spend too much time working and not enough time loving on your dog. Peacock? Is that anything to do with the club?"

"My brother and I own Peacock," Jem said.

"It was your brother who was shot. I'm sorry to hear about that."

Jem swallowed around the sudden lump in his throat. Even hearing it out loud was hard to listen to. Griff drew Jem to his feet and put an arm around him, and Jem gratefully accepted the comfort.

"He's going to be fine," Griff said.

Rob smiled at Jem. "That's good to hear. I'll leave you to

it. Message me when you need me to take care of your slobbery mutt." But the smile he bestowed on her, and the scratch behind the ears which made her eyes close in ecstasy, told Jem he was in Doris's thrall.

Griff encouraged Jem to sit on the couch and pet Doris while he called Quinn. It didn't escape Jem's attention that he walked out of the room to hold the conversation. Obviously Griff did not want Jem to hear what he had to say about his brother. The discussion went on longer than Jem expected, and he was almost dozing when Griff returned.

He opened his eyes to hear Griff coaxing a reluctant Doris off the couch.

"You need exercise," Griff told Doris pointedly, who ignored him and buried her nose in the crook of Jem's elbow. "Now you're just being annoying."

"She doesn't want to walk?" Jem yawned, his jaw clicking painfully.

"Doris prefers eating, sleeping, and cuddling to going for a walk." Griff threw up his hands. "What am I going to do with you?"

Doris yawned at him.

Then Jem's stomach rumbled. His cheeks heated but Griff nodded approvingly.

"Okay, I'll make food first. How about grilled cheese and tomato soup?"

Jem's belly rumbled again. "I think you got your answer."

Griff laughed and headed to the kitchen. Jem hesitated for a moment, then followed him.

"Do you have something a boy could eat with?" he asked hesitantly.

Griff had been head down, searching through a cabinet.

But he turned to face Jem. "I do. Plates and bowls and cups. Is that what you want?"

It was embarrassing to admit just how much Jem needed it. But in his heart, he knew Griff wouldn't think less of him, or make fun of him for asking for boy time.

Griff nodded. "Why don't you get changed into your PJ's, and then you can come sit at the table. Would you like to play with toys or color while I make the food?"

"Could I just sit with Doris? I'm really tired." Jem didn't want to think, didn't want to do anything, except stroke the dog, eat, and go to sleep, hopefully in Griff's arms.

Griff came over and kissed the top of his head. "You can do anything you want to do," he assured him. "Go change," and he patted Jem on the butt.

Jem wandered into the bedroom, with Doris following him. He looked down at the dog. "What am I doing, Doris? Am I making a big mistake here?" He laughed at Doris's snort. "Well of course you're going to say that. He is your master." Jem swore if Doris had been human she would have rolled her eyes at him.

He slipped out of the sweater and dress pants and shoes, not sure where to place them. He hung the pants over the chair and placed the shoes underneath. He groaned as he stretched tired muscles and redressed in the dinosaur T-shirt and shorts.

Jem padded back to the kitchen to find Griff whistling as he made the grilled cheese. The smell was incredible and for a moment Jem was taken back to spending Christmas with his grandmother.

"Feeling better?" Griff asked. He looked over his shoulder to give Jem a smile.

"Much," Jem confessed. He felt self-conscious wearing

a T-shirt and shorts when Griff was still dressed for the day. But Griff didn't seem to see anything odd in it.

"Where's Doris?" Griff asked.

Jem looked around but the dog was nowhere to be seen. "She followed me into the bedroom."

Griff groaned. "She'll be buried under the blankets by now. Doris likes to go to bed early and gets very upset if I don't join her. She'll be snoring by the time we go to bed."

Jem hugged that 'we' to himself. It came out sounding naturally and he wasn't sure Griff was even aware of it.

"Sit down at the table," Griff ordered.

Jem looked at the table and blinked. Griff had placed two bowls there. One of them china, and the other one was a plastic bowl with trains on it. He'd added a plastic cup of milk.

Griff gave him a steady gaze. "Usually I would negotiate all this before we start. But I know you're exhausted. All you have to do is eat your food, and we can relax after dinner. You can ask for whatever you want. It doesn't mean to say I'm going to say yes straightaway, but you can ask."

Jem nodded. He knew what he wanted, but Griff was right. He was tired and stressed and he probably needed a day or two to think about his needs when he wasn't tied up in knots worrying about his brother.

"Sit down."

Jem obeyed, and waited for Griff to bring the food to the table. His stomach rumbled happily at the thought.

The tomato soup looked delicious, and he hadn't had grilled cheese for years.

"Would you like me to cut up your sandwich?" Griff asked.

Jem hesitated, but he had asked for Griff to treat him like a boy, and this was part of it. He hadn't had this since his first Daddy. Eric Strada hadn't considered nurturing him as part of his role.

"Jem?"

Jem looked up, realizing he hadn't answered Griff's question. "Yes, please, Daddy."

Griff looked pleased. "When we're in a session, I want you to call me Daddy."

Jem nodded. He could do that. He'd like to call him Daddy all the time.

Griff cut up the grilled cheese into bite-size pieces, just right for a boy, and then he sat down to join him at the table.

Jem felt something nudge his legs, and he looked down to see Doris staring up at him hopefully. "You came back to find us, girl."

"She came back to try her luck," Griff groused. "She's not allowed any treats."

Jem thought that was a little unfair, particularly as he had the dog pleading with him, but he didn't want to upset his Daddy on their first session together.

He took the plastic spoon and dipped it into the soup. He was finally a boy.

Griff

He spent the dinner time ensuring Jem was as comfortable as he could be. He knew it had taken a lot for Jem to ask for what he wanted, and Griff wouldn't embarrass him for a moment. It took Jem a while to adjust to the plastic flatware and cutlery, but by the end of the meal he looked relaxed and happier than Griff had ever seen him.

Griff was careful to keep the conversation to neutral topics, letting Jem guide the conversation, and it inevitably focused on Doris. Jem was irrevocably in love with his dog.

Griff was resigned to the fact that Doris had claimed another victim in her quest to love the world.

Jem finished the cup of milk and left a milky white moustache on his top lip. Griff grabbed a paper towel and held Jem's chin. Jem startled a moment but then let Griff wipe away the milk.

"I expect my boys to help me clear away," he told Jem.

Jem nodded. Griff knew that Jem wasn't a brat, unlike Mo's boy. But he hoped as Jem got more comfortable with him that he would push Griff's boundaries. That was part of the fun of having a boy.

Once everything was in the dishwasher, much to Doris's disappointment, Griff looked at Jem. "What would you like to do next?"

"I'd like a bath and then to go to bed, Daddy," Jem said.

Even his voice sounded younger, with less of the strain that had been showing over the past couple of days.

"I'll give you a bath," Griff agreed.

He knew that was another big leap for Jem. He trusted Griff when he would be most vulnerable, and that was a gift Griff would not abuse. He would like to know why Jem trusted him after years of avoiding Daddies in the community. What had changed?

He held out his hand and Jem took it, then he led Jem into the bedroom. The bed was a mess as Doris had obviously been under the covers.

"She's a nightmare," Griff huffed as Jem chuckled.

"She's got you wrapped around her paws."

"Yes, she does," Griff admitted.

Doris leapt on the bed again and Jem sat down next to her to scratch her head.

Griff went into the bathroom to start the water running in the tub. He added bubble bath and toys. It wouldn't take long to run, as he used less water when it was for a boy than when it was for an adult. When it was ready, he rolled up his sleeves and tested the water carefully with his elbow. It wasn't too hot for his boy.

He dried his arm and hands and then went in search of Jem. He smiled to see Jem crooning at Doris who was rumbling happily along with him.

"Time for your bath." He could see the worry on Jem's face. "You don't have to do this if you don't want to. You don't have to do anything if you're not ready."

Jem scrambled off the bed. "I'm ready, but just take it slowly."

"I can do that," Griff assured him.

He took Jem's hand and led him into the bathroom. Jem blinked at the ducks bobbing along through the bubbles in the tub.

"I don't think I've ever played with toys in the bath."

"We can find other toys you want to play with another time," Griff said.

"Thank you. You're being really kind to me."

Griff saw Jem's eyes fill with sudden tears. He bent and kissed Jem on the cheek. "You deserve someone being kind to you."

Jem nodded, pressing his lips tightly together.

Griff tugged at Jem's T-shirt and pulled it over his head, then slid his fingers beneath the waistband of the shorts, feeling Jem's muscles contract. He slid it down Jem's legs, feeling the slight dusting of hair. Jem had a little soft, dark body hair, a slight patch under his arms and around his cock, and fine hair on his arms and legs. He ignored the way Jem's cock was obviously interested in Griff's presence. This was his time to be a boy.

Griff helped Jem into the tub. Jem sank down into the

water and sighed happily. One of the rubber ducks bobbed up to greet him and he giggled. He sounded so much like a young boy that Griff's heart soared in pleasure.

He let Jem play for a few minutes as he tidied away the pajamas and made sure there was a fresh towel for Jem when he got out of the bath. He didn't take his eyes off Jem though. He wanted to make sure Jem felt safe around him, and he wasn't going to leave him alone when he was vulnerable.

Then it was time to wash him. He grabbed a washcloth, one with dinosaurs, from a pile and knelt by the tub.

Jem squinted at the pile. "Could I have that one?"

Griff looked and saw Jem pointing to a purple one. He picked it up and looked at the picture. Was it the color or the pretty princess Jem liked? He scooped up a handful of bubbles with it.

Jem giggled. "This is fun, Daddy."

Griff returned his smile. "I'm glad you're enjoying it. I'm going to wash you now."

Jem closed his eyes obediently as Griff wiped at the last trace of milk on his top lip, then wiped the rest of his face. Griff used the bubbles to clean him, around his neck and down his arms. Scrubbing underneath his arms made him giggle, and he discovered Jem was ticklish. Griff filed that away for another time. Then he washed Jem's back and front. Another day he would take longer, but today he just wanted Jem clean and warm and ready for bed.

Griff washed Jem's cock and balls, ignoring Jem's blush and the way Jem's dick strained to meet him, and assured him this was part of his job.

He knew Jem was probably nervous after what had happened with his first Daddy, but he wanted Jem to know this was all normal. Then it was onto his legs and his feet where Jem giggled again.

"You really are ticklish." Griff grinned.

"So would you be if someone was rubbing your feet," Jem muttered.

"I'm not ticklish," Griff said. It wasn't quite true, but he would leave Jem to find that out for himself.

He heard Jem grumble something under his breath and he raised an eyebrow.

Jem hung his head. "I'm sorry, Daddy."

"I'm not going to ask what you said this time. But I don't expect you to be rude to me," he said sternly.

"Yes, Daddy."

"Let's get you out of the tub."

Griff stood and held out his hand. Jem scrambled to his feet and Griff helped him out onto the mat. He'd found a large towel which he wrapped around Jem and patted him dry. He took his time making sure Jem was dry in all corners.

Jem yawned and apologized. "I'm sorry, Daddy. It's been a long day."

"It has," Griff agreed. "Let's get you into your pjs, and you can go to bed."

"Are you coming with me?"

Griff wasn't sure whether Jem was worried about him coming or not coming. "I'm going to tidy up and then make sure Doris has a quick walk."

"You won't be long?"

"I'll only be a few minutes," Griff assured him.

When Jem was tucked up in bed, he fixed up the bathroom and let the water out of the tub. Then he whistled to a very reluctant Doris who was curled up with Jem.

"Come on, Miss Doris. You know the routine," he chided her.

Jem's mouth curled into a sweet smile. "You know Doris is the most spoiled dog ever."

"I know that, but she deserves it. She had a horrid start in life and deserves all the love we can give her."

"I like that you said we," Jem said.

"I like that too. See if you can get some sleep. I'll walk Doris around the block, and I'll be back in ten minutes."

"Thank you for taking care of me, Daddy." Jem's whisper was almost too quiet for Griff to hear.

But he did hear it and Griff smiled. "It's been a long time since I've had a special boy to take care of. Thank you for putting your trust in me."

He kissed Jem on the lips and pointed to the floor at Doris, who huffed and slowly slid off the bed, taking her time to finally get all four paws on the ground.

"You're such a drama queen," he muttered to her as they walked to the front door. Her smug expression was obvious.

He put on his jacket and grabbed her leash. He'd promised Jem he would be back in ten minutes. And he intended to keep that promise.

Chapter Eleven

Jem

Jem didn't relax until he heard Griff come back into the apartment, grumbling at Doris for taking her time. They were like an old married couple, although he'd never tell his Daddy that.

But now Griff was back, and Jem could sleep. He closed his eyes and burrowed down into the covers. It had been one helluva day. But at least his brother was going to be all right, and the cops should be off his back once they'd spoken to Max. He imagined Max was going to be in a lot of trouble with CDR once he was well enough to handle it. That would be Max's problem.

Jem had his own issues to deal with, including learning how to be a boy again. It had been so many years since he'd gotten into the boy mindset. He'd never really had a chance with Eric Strada. His earlier meal with Griff had been... interesting. He knew from Griff's careful comments that Griff had not been talking to him as he would one of his boys. He was grateful for that, not sure he could have handled it tonight. But he needed to learn. Maybe this was a conversation he could have with Louis. Quinn's boy, Cade, was too young, and besides which was always working too hard. Maybe he could have a play date with Louis. He knew Joseph was still learning, but he was also young. Although it would be good to be with someone who felt as out of place as he did. He didn't know Joseph except on a business basis. Maybe Griff could talk to Mo. Jem furrowed his brow. Maybe he should get up and make notes. There were so many things to think about.

"Hey, you're still awake," Griff said, sitting on the bed beside him.

Doris hauled herself up with a grunt and lay down the other side of him. Jem was effectively trapped.

"I couldn't relax until you were back," Jem admitted. "And I've been thinking about being a boy. Do you think I could have a play date with Louis?" He didn't expect the broad smile that spread across Griff's face.

"I think Louis would love that. He's feeling lonely among all the boys. They are a lot younger than he is. I think he would love to play with someone who is a similar age to him. But you know Joseph is still a newbie. He would probably like to talk to you."

"He was next on my list," Jem said. "I don't really know him. Max tended to deal with him more than I did. He said he was a nightmare."

"I think he's calmed down now he's got a Daddy of his own. I'll give Mo a call tomorrow and set up a play date. I warn you though, Joseph really likes his trains. He's addicted to them."

Jem had heard that Joseph used a train as a comfort blanket. He'd found it odd, but it seemed to calm him down, and he would never knock a boy for what suited him.

"I haven't played with train sets for years. Maybe Joseph would show me what to do."

"I just hope Mo has taught him how to share," Griff said.

Jem wanted to get away from the subject of toys. He was still struggling with the idea of sitting on the floor and playing. He had toys of his own, but they were in the apartment above the club and definitely not for small boys. He wondered when he'd get a chance to show them to Griff.

"Are you coming to bed?"

"Gonna take a quick shower and I'll be there," Griff promised.

He got up and went into the bathroom without kissing Jem, who missed the brief touch. It was strange, but even in the short time he'd been in Griff's company, he was used to Griff holding his hand and kissing him.

Jem sighed and scratched behind the dog's ears. Doris rumbled happily. "I think I'm falling for your Daddy," he said to her.

Doris grunted her agreement.

He was nearly asleep when Griff returned.

"End of the bed," Griff ordered.

Confused, Jem opened one eye to see Griff locked in a battle of wills with a reluctant dog. But finally Doris huffed and moved to the end of the bed. Griff got into bed and spooned around Jem, holding him close against his chest.

"Sleep tight, baby boy," Griff whispered.

Jem was aware of Griff's warm breath tickling the back of his neck, his strong arm around Jem, and his groin pushing against Jem's ass. Jem shivered at the thought of that solid shaft inside him, his dick hardening in anticipation.

"Are you cold?" Griff sounded concerned.

"No," Jem moaned.

"Then...oh." A warm hand slipped into Jem's sleep shorts and wrapped around his dick. "I thought you were sleepy."

Jem thrust up into Griff's hand. "I am but I need," he pleaded.

"Just my hand tonight."

Jem grumbled but when Griff took his hand away, he said quickly "I'm sorry, Daddy."

"Next time you're rude, you'll sleep in the playroom." But Griff slowly enfolded Jem's hard dick again.

Jem didn't say anything, desperate not to lose Griff's hand on him.

Griff stroked him, each tug making Jem's toes curl and push back against the rigid shaft pressing into his ass. He panted hard. Griff held him tighter, and his body was flush against Jem's. Just his sweet Daddy's hand was making Jem lose his mind.

"You feel so good, baby boy," Griff murmured.

Jem closed his eyes as his balls tightened. "Need."

He was reduced to one word, but his Daddy understood, stroking him harder and faster. Jem's focus narrowed down to his screaming need to climax and he yelled as he came hard, his cock pulsing, his come spilling over Griff's fingers.

He was still shuddering through his orgasm when he heard Griff grunt and warm stripes coated his ass.

They lay in the wreck of the bed for long moments before Griff pressed a kiss into the sweaty nape of Jem's neck.

"I didn't expect that. I'll get a washcloth and fresh pjs." Griff sounded as weary as Jem but he headed into the bathroom.

He returned, stripped off Jem's pajamas and tenderly cleaned him. Then he redressed him in fresh sleep shorts and a T-shirt.

They were cuddled up again when Jem said "What happened to Doris?"

Griff chuckled. "She's in her own bed, probably sulking. She's too much of a lady to watch."

Jem tilted his head and pressed a kiss under Griff's jaw. "Thank you."

"Thank you for trusting me, baby boy."

Jem closed his eyes and prayed that he hadn't given his trust too soon.

* * *

Jem was woken up by an unfamiliar ring tone. He struggled to consciousness as the noise stopped and Griff slid out of bed. He answered the phone and walked to the doorway.

"Quinn?"

It was Griff's tone that caught Jem's attention. It was sharp and without a trace of sleep. Jem struggled to sit up, Doris's heavy body next to him not helping.

"Yes, I'll let him know when he wakes up. Is he all right? What did they do?"

Jem's eyes were wide open. Any last trace of sleep was gone. It was obvious the conversation was to do with him. Was who all right? Max?

"Are the cops going to let us in?"

Jem pushed back the covers and rushed for the door. Griff started as he was only just outside. He held up his hand as Jem started to speak.

"Yes... Yes... No, don't worry. If we need to make a fast

exit we'll go to Mo's. The club can stay closed until the weekend."

Jem frowned. That was a decision that was down to him and Max, not Griff. He didn't like the way this conversation was going. He wanted to be Griff's boy, but that didn't mean Griff was going to make all the decisions for him, especially in his professional life. If that was what Griff expected, then it was better that they parted company now.

"I'll call you back in a few minutes. Jem is awake."

Griff disconnected the call and looked at Jem. "I'm sorry I disturbed you."

"What happened to Max?" Jem asked frantically.

"It's not Max. It's one of your bartenders. Cops got a call to your club. They found someone had broken in and he was on the floor unconscious."

"Who was it?" Jem demanded, frustrated by the lack of information.

"Pierre DuBois."

Jem put a hand to his mouth. "Oh my God. I saw him the night of the shooting. He was taking care of Conchita. You don't think Conchita was behind this, do you?"

"I don't know, Jem. This could be unrelated to the shooting. The club wasn't open last night. It might be opportunist."

"But why was Pierre there at all?" Jem stared at Griff. "There was no reason for Pierre to be at the club. It was still a crime scene. Detective Hamilton hadn't given me permission to reopen."

"I don't know. I wish I did. Quinn is at the hospital with Pierre. He's not happy because he doesn't want anyone near Max. If Pierre is involved, then both he and Max could be in danger."

Jem put his head in his hands. It was all too much. First

his brother, and now Pierre. Also the suggestion that Pierre was involved. He was a huge, sweet, flirty guy that the women loved and fluttered over. And he had always been loyal to the club.

Then strong arms came around him and Jem rested his face in the crook of Griff's neck, feeling the stubble rasp his cheeks. Griff stroked his head.

"It's okay. We'll find out what's going on."

"You keep saying that, but it just gets worse." Jem didn't mean to be ungrateful, but he was really tired of people telling him it was going to be okay.

Suddenly he heard his phone, and it was Max's ring tone. "I think Max has just found out the news."

Jem pulled away from Griff and jogged into the bedroom. His phone was in his pants pocket. He pulled it out and answered before it cut off.

"Jezza, have you heard about Pierre?" Max barked into the phone.

Jem pulled the phone away from his ear. The volume was too loud. "We just got the news. How did you hear?"

"Quinn called me."

Jem furrowed his brow. "Why was he calling you?"

"We had a heated discussion last night. Did you have to tell them about my nocturnal habits?"

"Yes, I did," Jem snapped. "That still doesn't explain why he called you at... What the hell time is it anyway?"

"It's just after seven. It's not that early. I'm going to see if I can find out what's going on with Pierre. What the hell was he doing at the club in the first place?"

"I have no idea. On my way over now."

"No, don't come anywhere near here. That's two of us they tried to kill. You could be next. Stay away from the club and stay away from the hospital."

"Like hell I will," Jem shouted. What the hell did Max think he was talking about? There was no way he'd stay away from the hospital.

Then the phone was plucked out of his hand. "Max, it's Griff. Is Quinn on his way over? And Craig? All good, then we'll take our time. No, I think you two need to have a serious discussion. It won't be dangerous with us there. Something is going on with your club, and you need to fix it now."

Griff

Jem looked betrayed at first until he realized that Griff was insisting they go over there. Griff squeezed Jem's shoulder as he disconnected the call.

"Max is just trying to protect you, but it's not going to help."

"Too right it's not," Jem said heatedly. "I don't know what he's thinking. Unless he's trying to hide something."

Griff gave a helpless shrug. "I'm really the muscle. It's my job to protect you. I leave other people to do the thinking. All I know is, keeping you away from your brother is not the best plan. You'll just fret."

Jem scowled at him. Maybe Griff's honesty wasn't the best idea. But then he gave a helpless shrug of his own.

"You're right, and I'm right too. God, it's too early. I need coffee."

Griff caressed Jem's cheek. "This wasn't how I planned things." In his head they'd had a quiet morning waking up, with another session where Jem could be in boy mode. He'd not intended to have the weight of the world on their shoulders before breakfast.

"Nor me," Jem said grimly.

"We'll pick this up later. For now we need to eat breakfast and get to the hospital." Griff held up his hand before Jem could protest. "You are going to eat something before we leave. Even if it's a bowl of oatmeal. I might not have time for pancakes today."

"I'd like oatmeal," Jem said in a meek voice.

Griff understood that Jem didn't want food, but he did want to please his Daddy. Griff could live with that.

He kissed Jem's forehead which immediately calmed him. "Good boy."

Jem grimaced. "I'm not sure how I feel about the good boy. My grandmother used to say that to their dog."

"We'll work on that one," Griff promised.

He shoved Jem toward the bedroom door and told him to have a shower. He was going to start the oatmeal. Doris snuffled anxiously at his feet and he realized he'd forgotten about his dog. He knelt on one knee and petted her, promising her breakfast as soon as he'd gotten the oatmeal on. She would have to spend the day with Rob again. His phone was still in his hand so Griff sent Rob a message. The response was instantaneous.

"Don't worry about walking her. I'll do that in fifteen minutes."

Griff gave a long sigh and patted Doris on her head. "You really are a lucky girl. Uncle Rob will be here soon." Her ears pricked up and she whined. Maybe he ought to think about giving her to Rob. Griff could be the fun uncle. It would make a change to be the interesting one.

By the time Jem returned from the shower, the oatmeal was in bowls. This time he hadn't used a plastic bowl. But he caught Jem looking at the china bowls, and he looked disappointed.

"I didn't want to presume. We hadn't talked about this being a session."

His explanation seemed to soften the blow for Jem.

"I would be happy to always have my boy's bowls, although I think I need coffee this morning," Jem admitted.

Griff inclined his head. "This is how we're going to do it. While you're staying here you will always get boys' bowls and cups. I have a cup that I can put your coffee in. The only time it will change is if outsiders are here. We can share this with Quinn and Craig and Mo and their boys, not other members of CDR."

"I agree to that," Jem said quietly. "I don't think I'm ready to show that side of myself to the outside world yet. Although Jace and Padraig seem so relaxed around you all."

"It's been intense for them. But they were used to mainly doing escorts for high-profile clients. Then suddenly they're dropped into the Daddy community, and there are all sorts of psychos around. They haven't had time to think about it."

Griff had really been only on the fringes of the Biker Daddy Bodyguards, by his choice, but now he realized there was a need for people like him. And Jace and Doug and Padraig. They were all needed.

"Eat your oatmeal before it gets cold, boy." He handed Jem a purple plastic spoon.

Jem sighed happily. "Purple is my favorite color."

Griff filed that for future reference. He didn't have much in the way of purple things. But that could change.

They were halfway through the oatmeal when Jem suddenly froze, a spoon almost to his mouth. Griff raised an eyebrow.

"Is something wrong? More wrong," he amended.

"The cops aren't going to think I had anything to do with Pierre, are they?"

"It's a fair question, but I can't see how. I'll be able to prove you were with me all night."

Jem gave him a steady look. "And how are you going to do that?"

"I have CCTV. Don't worry, they won't get any footage that I don't want them to see. But I can prove that you didn't move outside the bedroom."

"I could have organized a hit."

Griff rolled his eyes. "I don't think anyone's going to think you did that, boy."

"People always make the mistake of underestimating the quiet ones," Jem pointed out.

"Are you trying to make yourself look guilty?" Griff said, with a touch of exasperation.

"No, but I'm just trying to see it from their point of view. They already want to blame me for Max's shooting."

"I think you'll find their attitudes have changed somewhat."

Now it was Jem's turn to raise an eyebrow. "Why would they do that?"

"Because the more evidence they try to find on you, the more the evidence steers them in a different direction."

"I've never been so grateful to be a good boy." And then he flushed, suddenly realizing what he'd said.

Griff leaned forward. "I'm very grateful you're a good boy too, but I don't mind if you have a touch of the bad boy sometimes." He saw Jem's eyes go wide. Message received and hopefully understood.

"Okay, I think we have to go. Let's clear away everything."

Jem helped him clean up the breakfast things and then said he'd cuddle Doris while Griff had a shower.

When Griff returned to the main room, he discovered Rob sitting down talking to Jem, with Doris between them like she owned them. They appeared to be in a heated discussion about gin, of all things. Griff couldn't take his eyes off Jem and how animated he was. He was used to Jem being calm and laid back about the club, but for some reason he had strong opinions on flavors of gin. It didn't help when Rob called him a heathen. Then Griff discovered that Jem was a master when it came to gin and was prepared to shove Rob's opinion where the sun don't shine.

If it hadn't been for the fact that they had to go, he would have let Jem tear Rob into shreds, but they needed to move.

"I think you're outgunned there," he pointed out to his next-door neighbor.

"I think I am," Rob said ruefully.

Jem sat there with a calmer, smug smile. "You gentlemen seem to forget I've been in the business a long time."

"I won't make that mistake again," Rob assured him.

Griff smirked at him, then said goodbye to Doris who nuzzled him. Maybe she did love him after all. Then he watched her love all over Jem and decided he'd been a bit optimistic.

Jem was quiet in the car as they drove the short distance to the hospital.

"What's bothering you?" Griff asked.

"I've been thinking about you and me."

Griff's heart sank. He really hoped that didn't mean Jem wanted to give up on their relationship before it had even started.

"If, when, we sort everything out, I need to know that you respect my authority in my job. Peacock is half my club, and I've given my life to it."

Griff frowned at Jem's flat tone. "Where is this coming from?"

"You told Quinn that the club would stay closed until the weekend. That's not your decision. That should be my choice if the police say we can open up. I can't have you making decisions like that without discussing it with me first."

Jem refused to look at him, just staring out of the window. Griff focused on the road ahead. He hadn't even thought about it. He had just been making plans as his job entailed.

"Okay, that was high-handed of me. I was thinking of your safety, not of your business. In future, we'll have these discussions first."

"Thanks."

"But," Griff warned, "my job is to keep you safe and if that means keeping you away from the club, that's what I'll do. It's my job."

"I can't agree to that."

Chapter Twelve

Jem

The silence went on forever. Jem was afraid to turn around and look at Griff, not wanting to see the anger in his eyes. Was this where it ended? Before it had even begun? Jem thought about it for a long time. He couldn't hand over control of his business to his Daddy. It was too important to him. The Peacock club had been in his family for too long. Besides which, there was no way Max would let an outsider make decisions, even one as important as Griff.

They were almost at the hospital before Griff spoke.

"Now I know how Quinn, Craig, and Mo felt." He almost sounded amused.

Jem turned to look at Griff and saw the rueful smile on his face. "What do you mean?"

"The Daddy bodyguards deal with high-powered boys. It's a very difficult line to tread. You guys are used to taking control, and so are we. I've listened to all three of them bitching about it and thought they just needed to go all

Daddy on their boys' asses. Now I know how they feel. They're going to laugh their asses off."

Jem thought about Cade, Louis, and Joseph. None of them could be considered sweet, gentle boys. He was probably the closest, but he was still a businessman of a highly successful club. And he had said no to his Daddy. Another time he might have hyper- ventilated. Now he just had to take a deep breath and deal with it.

"How did they handle it?"

"Very carefully. Well, not Mo, because he wouldn't understand carefully if it bit him on the ass. But there's always negotiation involved. Let's start negotiating here."

"Okay," Jem said warily.

"I won't interfere in your decisions about the club. That's up to you and Max."

Jem breathed a little easier. He did not want to get between his brother and his Daddy.

"If I think your life is in danger at any point, I'm removing you from the situation. And if that means removing you from the club, I'm going to do that." Griff flicked Jem a quick glance. "That bit is nonnegotiable."

"But once we find out who shot my brother then it will be all over, won't it? I won't need you as my bodyguard again."

Griff grunted.

"What does that mean?" Jem asked suspiciously.

"It means that we'll see. I'm not making any decisions until this situation is all over. Your safety is paramount to me."

"As my Daddy or as my bodyguard?"

"Both. My Daddy side wants to lock you up in my apartment and never let you out."

Jem squashed the part of him which found that very hot, and asked, "And your bodyguard side?"

"Wants to lock you up in my apartment and never let you out."

"I think you might have an issue with possessiveness."

"Only with you," Griff admitted quietly. "I've never felt like this about any boy before, not even Lee."

Jem's heart soared at the admission. He'd never had anyone feel like this about him before, either. "I don't think locking me up is a good idea, but having you at my back is something I am very happy with."

"I'd rather have you on my lap."

"I want that too," Jem said, somewhat breathily.

Griff grinned at him. "You're probably the first boy I looked after to say so."

"Some boys like making a fuss for the sake of it."

"They do. Here we are. Let's go find out what's happened to Pierre and your brother."

Jem went to get out of the car, but Griff stopped him with a hand around his neck and tugged him close.

"I don't mind a little fuss," Griff admitted.

Jem swallowed. "I'll remember that."

Then Griff kissed him. It was awkward, the angle wrong, and Griff's stubble rasped across his chin. But Jem didn't want it to stop. He could have stayed in the car like this for ever.

Griff let him go with a slight smirk. His Daddy was pleased with himself. Bastard. But Jem grinned as he got out of the car.

They heard Max shouting again before they got anywhere near his room.

"He's gonna make himself unpopular if he keeps doing that," Griff pointed out.

"If he gets to be too much they can sedate him," Jem said.

Griff barked out a laugh. "I can see you've thought about that before."

"More than once," Jem admitted. "My brother is always loud."

"You're not kidding," someone said behind them.

They turned to see Doug grimacing at them. "It's been like this for an hour. They made the mistake of telling him that your bartender had been brought in."

"I'll go calm him down," Jem said. "Which idiot told him?"

"That would be me," Quinn said as he emerged from Max's room.

Quinn was three times Jem's size and scared the living bejesus out of him, if Jem was honest with himself. But now, he was just a pain in the ass. Jem glared at him. "What did you do that for?"

"I wanted to see his reaction."

Jem waved a hand in the air. "Well, you got it. And I'm gonna have to calm him down."

He stalked into the hospital room to find Max trying to get out of bed, and Louis and Craig pressing him down.

"Get the fuck off me," Max snapped.

"Quit making a fuss," Jem said. "They just want to stop you killing yourself, you idiot."

"And where the hell were you?"

Jem glared at his brother. He wasn't going to be the bad guy in this scenario. "Not at the club because it was a crime scene." Max stopped struggling and laid back against the pillows. Jem had a feeling the energy had suddenly drained out of him. He looked around the room at everyone, and then at Griff. "Can everyone get out of here for a moment. I need to talk to Max. Griff, can you find out what's happening with Pierre?"

He saw the conflict in Griff's eyes. Griff didn't want to leave him alone.

"I'll go find out what's happening with Pierre," Craig said. "Griff should stay here. Louis, come with me. Quinn, go get coffee."

Jem was amused at the way Quinn's face changed when he was given an order, but to Jem's surprise, he didn't argue.

Once the room had emptied, including Griff who said he would stand outside the door, Jem looked at Max.

"How do you feel?"

"Fucking awful," Max admitted.

He looked dreadful. His face was ashen, but with bright red patches on his cheeks, and his eyes looked feverish.

Jem went to the door and beckoned to Griff, who was with him in an instant. "I think Max is running an infection, which may be one of the reasons he's such an asshole at the moment. Can you get a nurse to take a look at him?"

Griff nodded. "Leave it to me."

Jem went back to Max who was lying with his eyes closed. "Let's just calm down for a few minutes before we have to face everyone."

Max didn't open his eyes as he said, "You know telling me to calm down is a waste of time."

"I know, but you're starting to freak everyone out."

"Including you?"

"Not really. I'm used to you yelling."

Max opened his eyes. "I never yell at anyone."

Jem snorted. "Your nose just got bigger when you lied."

He chuckled at the offended look on Max's face, but he

was pleased to see his brother returning to his normal self. He would be having words with the guys about their high-handed attitude.

A nurse bustled in with a large smile on her face. She surveyed the patient in the bed. "I think we need to take some vitals." She turned to Jem. "You can wait outside."

"He can stay with me," Max growled.

Jem got to his feet before she could respond. "Do what the nice nurse says, and I'll bring you coffee."

Max glowered at him. "Just how I like it? It better not be from a vending machine."

"As if I would be that stupid or cruel."

The nurse raised one eyebrow. "Do I get one too for putting up with him?"

Ignoring Max's growl, Jem grinned at her. "Give me your order."

He left Max in the nurse's hands and rejoined Griff outside the room. "I have coffee orders."

"You'd better give them to me," Louis said. "Quinn's been called off to somewhere or another."

"That's convenient," Jem muttered, but he passed on the order.

Griff had a frown on his face and, when Louis was gone, Jem turned to him. "What's going on?"

"Craig and Quinn got called down to the ER. I'm sorry to have to tell you but it doesn't look good for Pierre."

Jem swayed and Griff placed a hand around his back. "It's okay, I've got you."

"I thought he just got knocked unconscious," Jem whispered.

"He's had a subdural hematoma. They need to get him into surgery immediately."

Overwhelmed by the shitstorm his life had become, Jem

pressed his face into Griff's chest. "What the hell is going on?"

Griff

Griff watched Jem closely. Jem was deep in conversation with Detective Hamilton, who had reluctantly conceded that Jem was no longer their prime suspect.

Pierre was hanging on by a thread. They were all confused as to why Pierre had even been at the club when it had been closed for two days. Now it seemed the cops had a lead, thanks to a chip in one of Pierre's pockets. An anonymous tipoff had led them to an illegal gambling den. It seemed that Pierre was a regular customer. Detective Hamilton was trying to find out if Jem knew anything about it.

Griff hung back while Hamilton talked to Jem, but if the detective upset his boy, there would be words.

"We don't have gambling in the club," Jem insisted. "We never have allowed it. We don't have a license for gambling."

"You don't have lock-ins?"

Jem gave Hamilton a cool look. "You know we don't. Peacock has always complied with the law."

Griff had never been a clubber or worked at the club before he met Jem, but he had to agree, he hadn't seen any sign of illegal activity while he'd been there. He knew from Louis that Peacock preferred to remain an exclusive club rather than the next hot thing. Much as Romero did.

Hamilton grunted. "I'm going to need to talk to your brother."

Jem looked reluctant, but now there had been a second

attack, the situation was more serious. "Okay, but don't wear him out. He's fighting an infection."

"I'll keep it as brief as possible," Hamilton said.

Jem led Hamilton to Max's room, Griff trailing them. Max had his eyes closed when they went in but, as he opened them, Griff was sure he flinched at the sight of Detective Hamilton.

"Is Pierre—"

"He's still hanging on," Jem assured him. "Detective Hamilton needs to talk to you about something he found in the club."

Max nodded. "I've been waiting for you to ask."

Griff narrowed his eyes. That was an odd way of phrasing it. What had Max been waiting for? Judging from Jem's frown, he'd noticed it too.

The cop turned to Jem and Griff. "I need to talk to your brother alone."

"But—" Jem protested.

Griff fixed his gaze on Jem. "We need to leave them alone to talk. We'll wait outside. Detective, do you want me to send your partner in when she arrives?" Apparently Detective Mitchell had been held up in traffic.

"Yeah, thanks." He gave Griff a nod as if to say thank you for handling Jem too.

Griff guided Jem out of the room. As soon as the door was shut, Jem turned on him.

"I should be in there with him. He needs my support."

"Hamilton is just asking him a few questions."

Jem shook his head. "You don't believe that any more than I do. You heard what Max said."

"Max is still stoned."

"Then he shouldn't be interviewed without someone else present."

Jem looked as if he was about to burst back into Max's room when Mitchell approached and nodded at Jem.

"Mr. Peacock."

"Detective," he said, his voice icy.

"I'm looking for Detective Hamilton."

"He's in there," Griff said, pointing at the door.

She smiled at them and entered Max's room without knocking.

Jem did not look happy. Griff took Jem's hands in his and placed them over his heart.

"Max is in good hands."

"They thought I'd shot Max," Jem pointed out acerbically.

"Hamilton did, yeah. But I did some investigation into him. He's a good cop. By the book. And he's prepared to admit when he gets it wrong."

"Which he did."

"Which he did," Griff agreed.

"What has Max gotten himself into?" Jem whispered.

Griff focused all his attention on Jem. "We don't know. Don't worry until we know the full story. It could be something as simple as him knowing Pierre liked gambling."

"Max used to gamble."

The admission was dragged out of Jem as if it were shameful.

"Used to?" Griff asked carefully.

"He became addicted to gambling. We nearly lost the club because of him. I made him go to rehab, and we changed the financial controls at the club so he couldn't gamble it away."

With a surge of pride, Griff realized that, under his gentle exterior, Jem had a spine of steel. But now he needed to talk to Quinn and Craig. This put a new light on the situation.

"Do you think you should talk to your uncle? Max might need a lawyer."

Jem nodded. "I'll call him now." He turned to walk away and then looked back at Griff. "Do you think Pierre might need a lawyer too?"

"Let's see if he lives first," Griff suggested.

Jem's mouth tightened but he nodded again. He walked away, pulling his phone out of his pocket as he did so.

Griff watched him call his uncle, then he placed a call to Quinn.

"Ryder."

"It's Griff. We've got a new development."

"Go on."

"The cops found a chip in Pierre's pocket. Jem has just informed me that Max is a gambling addict, so Max could be involved in something that we don't know about."

"That matches up with the report we've just received," Quinn said.

"Oh?"

"Doug went around some of the other clubs in the area. It seems Max strays from Peacock on a regular basis. He's been seen with other men."

"So the guy is gay. That's hardly a crime."

"The men he's with are not interested in where you stick your dick," Quinn said. "These guys are more interested in where you stick your knife."

"Shit." Griff really hoped this was not true.

"Dominic's put some other guys onto this. I'll tell you as soon as I have any further information. How's Jem doing?"

"He's just found out that his big brother might be dirty. How do you think he's doing?"

"There might be an innocent explanation to all this."

"I really hope there is." Griff sighed.

"I've got to go. Dominic is losing his shit at somebody."

Griff snorted. "Another day ending in y then."

CDR's top dog was well known for his explosive temper.

Jem was just finishing his call. Griff waited until he had disconnected and put his phone in his pocket before he walked over. Briefly, he contemplated not telling Jem about the news from Quinn, but he swiftly decided against it. He wasn't going to start their relationship on the basis of lies.

"What did your uncle say?"

"He's on his way over. He's annoyed with me for allowing the police to interview Max without him present, but I pointed out that it wasn't like we knew anything." Jem looked at Griff. "What is it you aren't telling me?"

"Max has been seen in some less than savory company. We don't know anything more than that. When I do know, I'll make sure I tell you."

"Would you hug me?" Jem begged.

Griff wrapped his arms around Jem. He rested his cheek on top of Jem's head and almost rocked him. "It's all right, my boy. I'll take care of you."

"What's happening to us, Daddy?" Jem whispered.

Griff pulled him closer. "Just remember none of this is your fault. Whatever is going on, it has nothing to do with you."

"But Max is involved, isn't he?"

"It looks like it, but CDR has a lot of resources. We'll get to the bottom of it, I promise."

"Isn't that the cops' job?"

"We'll give them a helping hand." Griff was fully

prepared to make himself a pain in the butt if it meant he could look after his boy.

"What if Max has been involved in something illegal?" Jem asked, almost in a whisper.

Griff bent his head so he could whisper back in Jem's ear. "You're not on your own, boy. I'm here to look after you, to give you support. And if Max needs it, to give him support too."

"You and me," Jem said.

"You and me and Doris. Don't forget her. She'd be mortified if she was left out."

That produced a laugh from Jem, even if it was a shaky one. "How could I forget Miss Doris?"

They stayed where they were, Griff holding Jem tight. The nurses and assistants carried on with the business of the day, as if seeing two men clinging to each other was normal.

Griff looked up to see Daniel Peacock striding toward them, a grim look on his face. "Your uncle is here."

Jem raised his head. "Thank you for coming."

"Are the police still in with Max?" Daniel demanded, as if he had no time for leisurely greeting.

"Yes," Griff said.

Jem gave his uncle a worried look. "Do you know what's going on?"

Daniel's face darkened. "I'm afraid I do. I'm afraid I do."

Chapter Thirteen

Jem

Jem pulled away from Griff's arms. He couldn't focus when he was in his Daddy's embrace. "What do you mean? What's going on with Max, Uncle Daniel?"

"I'm afraid I can't talk about it, Jeremy. Not until Max gives me permission." Daniel's expression was bleak.

"Is he gambling again? Is that it?" Jem heard his voice crack, hating any sign of weakness.

"I need to talk to Max."

Jem narrowed his eyes, feeling the anger rise in him. He remembered what it was like before, when he had discovered the extent of Max's debts. "I won't be shut out like this. Max is my brother. If he's in trouble, I want to know about it."

Griff wrapped his arm around Jem's shoulders. Jem shook him off again. He needed to focus on Daniel.

"Just let me talk to Max," Daniel said, his expression softening. "I know you love your brother. I promise you I'll do everything I can to help him."

And then he was inside Max's room, leaving them behind. Jem was furious.

"I don't understand what's going on. If Max is in trouble, why is no one telling me?"

"We've only just found out that there is trouble," Griff pointed out. "That's more information than we had before."

"This isn't right."

Jem could feel the pressure building inside him. He was ready to explode at anyone, frustrated by the lack of information.

Griff pressed his lips together. "Boy, you're going to come with me."

"I can't leave Max."

Griff pointed to Craig who had just exited the elevator. "Craig is going to stay here and, if anything happens, he can call us."

"What am I going to do?" Craig asked.

"My boy needs a break," Griff said. "Daniel Peacock and the cops are in with Max. I'm going to take Jem home for a couple of hours. Can you stay here and, if anything happens, call me?" He emphasized the me.

Craig blinked at Griff and then he took a long look at Jem. "That's a good idea."

Jem shook his head. "No, I won't leave him."

Griff focused his attention on Jem. "Boy, you will come with me."

Jem hadn't heard that particular tone in Griff's voice before. He saw Craig's eyes widen. Craig looked as surprised as Jem felt. Jem had a feeling Griff was going to make him leave whether he wanted to or not. He was either going to have to go quietly or make a scene. "You promise to drive me back the second we hear something?"

"I do," Griff promised. "We'll go home, and you can

relax. I know how the cops work. It'll be hours before they finish. You remember how long it was before they let you go."

"But Max is injured."

"If he's well enough to make a fuss, he's well enough to be questioned by the police," Craig said brusquely. "Jem, listen to your Daddy. You will find out what's going on later. I will call you."

Jem deflated. "Yes, Daddy Craig." That was the first time he'd acknowledged Craig's Daddy status. The first time Jem had acknowledged he was a boy in public.

Jem found himself being shuffled away from Max's room, Griff's arm around his shoulders, and then he was in Griff's car.

"What happened to the elevator?"

Griff turned to look at him. "You blanked out, huh?"

"I must have."

"It's okay, boy. You're tired and overwrought. Don't worry. A couple of hours' break, and you'll feel well enough to start again."

"I didn't even ask about Pierre."

"He's still alive. Quinn is sending me regular updates. Pierre's family is there, and they've told Quinn that you're to focus on your brother. The situation looks a bit more hopeful now."

Jem bit his lip. "Make sure he gets anything he needs."

Griff pressed his lips together. "Before you make an offer like that, you need to find out if Pierre is involved. He might have been the one who shot Max."

"He would never. Pierre's a sweetheart."

"That's what Louis thought about the guy who tried to kill him. And Cade thought that about his driver," Griff pointed out. "Let's find out more information first."

"It must be awful to always think the worst of people," Jem muttered.

"Unfortunately, it's my job to be suspicious."

For one awful moment, Jem hated Griff for putting such suspicions in his mind, but then he sighed. "Where are we going?"

"I thought we'd go home, have a snack, and you can relax."

Jem was on the point of telling Griff that he wasn't hungry, but he was starting to realize that was futile. If Griff wanted him to eat, he would eat.

"Doris is going to be confused about seeing you home again."

"Doris will be with Rob. I'm going to leave her there. I'd like to spend time focusing on you. Just you."

Jem realized he desperately needed that too. "Can we go in the playroom?"

"Yes, we can. I'll read you a story."

Jem wasn't sure about the idea of being read a children's story, but he liked the idea of snuggling up to Griff in that big seat. He relaxed until Griff pulled into his space in the underground parking lot.

Griff cut the engine and smiled at him. "Come on. Just you and me for a little while."

Jem suddenly thought about something. It had been playing on his mind for a while, but he hadn't actually formulated it in his mind. "How can you be part of the Biker Daddy Bodyguards when you have a car?"

"I have a motorcycle too," Griff chuckled. He pointed to one corner of the parking lot where there was a line of motorbikes. "The old Hog on the end is mine. I usually ride her, but it seemed easier to transport you by car."

"Would you take me out on it—her—one day?" Jem asked.

"Do you like bikes?"

"I don't know. I've never been on one. But all the other boys seem to, so I'd like to try."

He saw how pleased Griff was and realized this was something important to his Daddy.

"We'll do that when all this is over," Griff agreed. He got out of the car, came around to open the door for Jem, then held out his hand. "Let me take care of you for a while."

Jem nodded. He needed his Daddy's care.

The apartment seemed empty without Doris rushing toward them. Jem stood inside the front door, his will to do anything for himself fading. He felt himself sinking into his boy mode. He wasn't in the mood to play. He just wanted to be taken care of.

Griff hung up his jacket, then turned to Jem, slipping his coat from his shoulders before hanging it next to Griff's. He knelt to unlace Jem's shoes and placed them in the hall closet.

"Do you want to eat first?"

Jem shook his head. "I'll eat later. Can we...can I sit on your lap please?"

Griff smiled at him tenderly. "I can do that. I want you to change into your pjs, then we'll go into the playroom."

Jem screwed up his courage and asked for the one thing he needed. "Can you change me please, Daddy?"

Griff

Griff recognized the change in Jem's voice as he slipped into his boy mode. "I can change you into your pjs." He noticed

Jem's hesitation. "What's wrong, my boy?" Concern shot through him as Jem refused to meet his gaze. "Jem, look at me," he ordered. Jem raised his head and Griff wanted to drown in his emerald eyes, but his boy looked so scared. Griff took his hands and Jem clutched them tight. "Talk to me."

"I want to wear..."

Jem ducked his head again, but Griff smiled, understanding what his boy needed. "You want to wear a diaper?"

Jem nodded. "Please. Just here. Not..."

Not outside the apartment. Griff understood. Jem seemed ashamed, and Griff couldn't have that. He grasped Jem's chin and raised his head so their gazes locked.

"Don't ever be embarrassed to ask for what you want. There's nothing shameful about wanting to wear a diaper."

"I've never...told anyone before."

"Not even your first Daddy?"

Jem bit his lip. "I didn't trust him."

Griff's heart melted. How had he been so lucky to find his boy? "Thank you for trusting me."

He guided Jem into the playroom and then into the closet with the changing mat. He could feel the tension in Jem. "Jem—"

"Jemmy," Jem said.

"Only when you're a boy?" Griff asked carefully.

His boy nodded.

"Okay, Jemmy. Would you like a pacifier?"

Jemmy nodded and Griff led him over to a drawer. He pulled it open and Jemmy peered in, before he finally pointed to a purple one.

"This one?" Griff asked.

"Yes, please, Daddy."

Griff could see the hope and need in his eyes. He

handed Jemmy the binky and saw the relief when he started to suck on it. He smiled at his boy. "Let's get you changed. Arms up."

Jemmy raised his arms and Griff tugged the sweater over his head, careful not to dislodge the binky. He undid the fastening of the dress pants and slid them down Jemmy's thighs. With each piece of clothing removed, Jemmy seemed to become more of a little.

"Good boy," Griff praised, running his finger around the waistband of the briefs with the cars.

Then he picked up Jemmy, who gave a muffled squeak, and placed him on the changing mat. "Lay down," he encouraged.

Awkwardly, Jemmy lay down on the mat, furiously sucking on the binky.

Griff picked up a diaper and with the ease of long experience stripped him of his briefs and diapered Jemmy, checking his face to make sure he wasn't freaking out.

Jemmy's gaze was fixed on him, his binky in his mouth, but now he wasn't sucking hard. Griff realized he wasn't freaking out. He was the calmest Griff had ever seen him. He was where he wanted to be.

Griff pushed a lock of dark hair back from Jemmy's face. "You're my little, my boy."

Jemmy pulled the binky from his mouth. "Tank oo."

"If you need to go potty wearing the diaper, you can," Griff assured him.

Jemmy nodded, a flush spreading across his cheeks.

"Nothing is taboo as long as we've agreed it beforehand."

Griff needed Jem—Jemmy—to understand he wasn't like his first Daddy. Nothing would happen that Jem didn't agree to, before he slipped into Jemmy. Even the discipline.

He would show his boy what it was like to be nurtured and loved.

But for now, they didn't have much time. He pulled a onesie from the shelf above. "Let's get you dressed, and we'll have cuddle time."

The onesie was a little big, but Jemmy didn't seem to mind, tracing the purple dinosaurs with one finger.

Griff lifted him off the changing mat and led him into the playroom. "Do you want to play, read, or just cuddle?"

"Cuddle please, Daddy."

The armchair was spacious enough for two large men. Griff sat down and drew Jemmy on top of him. Jemmy snuggled in with a contented sigh. Griff kissed the top of his head, then he reached out to an old CD player and switched it on. Nursery rhymes filled the room. He had music for all ages.

"Daddy?"

"Yes?"

"You won't tell anyone about this?" Jemmy sounded worried and too much like Jem.

Griff rocked him gently. "Baby boy, what happens here is between you and me."

"Not even the other Daddies?"

"Especially not the other Daddies," Griff assured him. "It's just you and me."

Jemmy's sigh was heartfelt, and he burrowed into Griff's chest. Griff stroked his head, feeling the silky hair under his palm.

"Daddy?"

"Yes, Jemmy?"

"Can I play with dolls?"

"Of course you can. Would you like to pick one to cuddle?"

Jemmy sat up and studied the line of dolls. Griff made sure he had all ages for his boys. Jemmy looked at Griff who nodded, then he clambered off Griff's lap and went to a pretty black baby doll dressed in a yellow lace dress.

"Bring it back here."

Griff held out his arms and Jemmy returned with the doll and sat back on Griff's lap, snuggling in, and hugging the dolly to him.

They sat in peace for a while as the CD continued. Griff watched Jemmy stroke the lace. He wasn't sure if Jemmy was even aware of it. "I have lots of clothes in the closet you can dress up in, including dresses," he said quietly.

He felt tension flood through Jemmy, and he expected a protest that Jemmy was a boy and didn't wear dresses. Jemmy stayed silent.

Griff kissed him again. "Whatever *you* want." He heard a sob and held Jemmy tight. How long had his boy been holding back his needs? If Jem would allow, Griff would dedicate his life to giving his love exactly what he needed. His love. Griff held Jemmy closer to him. Jem and Jemmy. His lover and his boy.

"I like playing dress-up," Jemmy said.

"I know other littles who do. We can arrange a playdate with them when you're ready." He smiled as Jemmy's belly rumbled. "I think we need to feed you."

"My tummy is rumbly." Jemmy sounded indignant.

"Let's go feed that rumbly tummy. You can bring the dolly with you."

Jemmy clutched the doll close. "Bridget. Her name is Bridget."

"Come on, Jemmy and Bridget. Let's feed you both."

While Jemmy sat on the couch, chattering to Bridget,

Griff sent a quick text to Craig. The response was immediate.

He's still with the cops. This is serious.

Fuck. Fuck. If Max went to jail, how would Jem cope?

"What's wrong, Daddy? You look worried."

Griff saw the concern in Jem's expression. He could tell the difference between Jem and Jemmy just by staring into his beautiful eyes. "It's all right, baby boy. Max isn't finished yet. We have time to eat."

Jem looked at Bridget and put her down on the couch next to the binky. "I don't think I can be a boy now."

He looked utterly defeated. Griff ached for him. He went over and knelt in front of him, concerned when Jem shrank back a little.

"You did so well, baby boy. This was our first session. There'll be plenty more."

Griff wasn't sure if he was reassuring Jem or himself.

"Are you sure?" Jem sounded withdrawn, so unlike the happy boy a few minutes previous.

"I am," Griff promised. "Why don't you stay in your onesie as it's comfortable. You can change before we go back to the hospital." He caught Jem eyeing Bridget. "We could put Bridget by our bed."

"You don't think she should go in the playroom? What if someone sees her?"

Oh, his boy just couldn't ask for what he needed.

Griff shook his head. "Our friends know who we are, and I think she'd be happiest sleeping with us, don't you?"

Jem's smile was tentative, but he hurried off to their bedroom with Bridget in his arms. Griff looked down at the pacifier. Maybe his boy wasn't ready to give up Jemmy so easily.

When Jem returned, Griff smiled at him. His boy

smiled but it didn't reach his eyes. Griff sought for something to cheer him up. "How about tomato soup and grilled cheese again?"

"You've been taking lessons from Daddy Craig."

Griff raised an eyebrow. "Oh?"

"When Louis was hurt, soup was all he could eat," Jem said.

"I like soup," Griff confessed. "I like making my own but today it will have to be canned soup again."

"That's okay with me."

Griff handed Jem his binky as he stood. "Take care of this."

Jem turned the pacifier over and over in his hand. "It felt so right."

"You looked so happy," Griff said, his smile gentle. "And that's what I want for you. To be happy."

"How do you know what I need, before I do?" Jem sounded somewhat frustrated.

"I've been a Daddy for a long time. I don't always get it right, but I'm good at reading body language."

"The dresses?" Jem asked, biting his lip.

"You touched the lace on a doll's dress."

"You're a boy whisperer."

Griff chuckled. Boy whisperer. He'd been called worse things. He could live with that.

Chapter Fourteen

Jem

Jem may not have been able to focus on being a boy, but he could act. He ate his lunch and smiled as if he were pleased at the praise from Griff. But inside he was dying. Griff had lied to him. His Daddy had lied to him. Jem didn't know why, but it obviously had something to do with Max. If he couldn't trust his Daddy to tell him the truth, then who could he trust? And he could see the worry on Griff's face. Something was seriously wrong with Max and he didn't know what it was. He'd tried to explain to Griff before, that Griff could not treat him like a child outside of their sessions. He was the co-owner of a respected club. His dream of being a boy 24/7 was just not practical now. And Griff obviously couldn't respect that.

He stared out of the window as they drove back to the hospital.

"Jem, are you all right?"

Jem turned to give him a sad smile. "I'm fine."

Griff frowned, but he didn't push the topic. Jem almost wished he did, and then he would have a chance to yell and shout. Instead, he ended up staring out of the window again until they arrived at the hospital.

Craig was where they'd left him, pacing up and down outside the closed door of Max's room. He looked relieved when he saw Griff and Jem approach. "The cops have just left. Your uncle is still in there with Max."

"Have they finished with him?" Jem demanded.

"I don't know," Craig said. "They weren't talking."

"What about Pierre?"

"The last report I got, he was still alive."

"I need to visit with him," Jem said.

"I could find out what's going on now you're here," Craig suggested.

Jem shook his head. He turned to Griff. "Will you find out what's happening with Pierre?"

Griff looked surprised, then wary. "I should stay with you. I'm your bodyguard."

"I'll be fine with Craig," Jem insisted.

Griff didn't look happy, but he did as he was asked, stalking away to the elevators.

Jem turned to see Craig glowering at him, his arms folded across his chest. He quailed at Craig's expression.

"Are you going to tell me what that's about?"

"I don't know what you mean," Jem said.

"Yes, you do. Why did you just send your protection detail away?"

Jem screwed up every bit of his courage. "I want a new bodyguard. It's not working out with Griff."

Craig's eyes narrowed and Jem felt as if he were a trapped butterfly being pinned to a board.

"You were fine when you left. What's happened since then? Did Griff hurt you?"

Only my heart.

"He didn't hurt me. It's just not working out for me. I need a regular bodyguard, not a Daddy."

"Jem—"

Jem gave him a defiant look. "I don't want to discuss it any further. If CDR can't find me a replacement bodyguard, then I'll look elsewhere. I'm going in to see my brother now. I'd like it organized by the time I come back out."

Jem walked away before Craig could discuss it further. He walked into Max's room without knocking on the door. He was not going to be put off from visiting his brother any longer, and he was going to find out what was going on with Max, whether Max liked it or not.

Max and Daniel were deep in conversation. They looked up as Jem entered, both with frowns on their faces at the unwanted interruption.

"We're not finished yet," Daniel snapped.

"I don't care. Tell me what the hell is going on," Jem said, just as forcefully.

"I can't tell you," Max said. "I don't want you involved."

"I *am* involved. I'm your brother, you idiot. Whatever it is, the club is involved now too. One of our bartenders is clinging to life downstairs, so tell me."

Jem stalked over to the bed and glared down at his brother, noting how worn-out Max looked, the pinched lines deep around his eyes and mouth, and his face so pale. He looked old and tired, but Jem's sympathy was limited.

"It's too dangerous." Max lay back on the pillows and closed his eyes as if he were blocking Jem out.

"You don't get to ignore me," Jem barked out fiercely. "If Uncle Daniel is here, then you can tell me." When Max didn't open his eyes, Jem leaned down and whispered in his ear. "Either you tell me, or you never walk back in the club again. We're done."

He expected Max to start yelling and protesting, but instead Max huffed and opened his eyes to fix his green gaze on Jem.

"I don't think I'll be coming back anyway."

"What do you mean?" Jem demanded, fear coursing through him.

Max looked over at Uncle Daniel. "He's got to know, Uncle Danny. I can't just walk out on him. He's my brother."

Daniel's face looked as pinched as Max's. "You're putting him in danger."

"I'm already in danger," Jem said. "And I'm not leaving without knowing the reason why my brother is about to walk out of my life."

He felt sick to the stomach, knowing whatever he was about to hear was going to change his life forever.

Max huffed and took Jem's hand in his. They both had slim hands with long slender fingers. "I started gambling again."

Disappointed to the core, Jem tried to pull his hand away, but Max hung onto it. "No wait, Jezza, you need to listen to me. This may be the only chance I get to tell you what's going on."

"You promised me you'd never gamble again. You promised," Jem hissed, tears prickling his eyes.

Max shook his head sadly. "It's an addiction, little brother. You know that. I was better. I gambled for minuscule amounts, and I didn't put the club at risk this time."

"But why?"

"Because I love the thrill, and nothing can replace it. If I wasn't so damn good at gambling, it wouldn't be a problem."

"You nearly lost us the club," Jem snapped.

"And this time, I didn't. But it was much, much worse."

Jem stared at his brother. "What could be worse? What did you do, Max?"

"It wasn't what I did, it was what I saw." Max went a strange shade of green. "I think I'm gonna barf."

Jem looked around and saw a basin, which he put by Max's side. "Keep talking," he said tersely.

Max scowled but he carried on. "I was at a poker game. I'm not gonna tell you where, since you won't approve. I stumbled out to the bathroom and I saw a man being killed." He swallowed hard. "I thought it was a dispute between two guys, but it was actually a hit. The guy was a fixer for the mob. I backed out quietly. I thought I wasn't seen. But then guys I gambled with started dying. All the other people at the game are dead, except for me."

"And Pierre," Jem said with a sudden revelation. "Pierre was at the game too."

Max looked startled. "No. He's a gambler, but he wasn't at the game."

Jem scowled at him. "So you and Pierre have been gambling? Who else has been involved from the club?"

"I don't think that's really the problem at the moment," Daniel murmured.

Jem turned on him, and Daniel took a step back. "This is *my* club, and my brother and my bartender have been screwing around. I want to know who else is involved."

Max licked his dry and cracked lips. "No one else, I promise you. I met Pierre at a game one night. He didn't know about my history, and I didn't know he gambled. He shouldn't be involved. He wasn't even at the game. I don't know why they're after him."

Jem turned on Daniel. "It's your turn. What have you got to do with this?"

"Max came to me for advice when he realized things were going so wrong." Daniel pursed his lips. "He ignored my advice, which was to go to the police."

"The cops want to put me into witness protection until they catch the guys doing this."

"For how long?" Jem asked in horror.

Max shrugged and then winced. "I don't know. But it's serious, Jem. Even the cops think they can't protect me."

Jem wrapped his arms around himself, feeling cold and scared. He desperately needed someone to hold him and tell him everything was going to be all right. But he just sent Griff away and now it looked as if nothing was ever going to be right again.

"When are you going?"

"As soon as they can arrange it." Max looked sadly at his little brother. "I'm so sorry, Jem. I am so sorry."

"And what about me? Do they think I'm in danger too?" Jem demanded.

"I don't think so," Daniel said. "Pierre regularly played in the poker games. The cops think he was a warning to Max. But you have no connection to gambling."

"I'm his brother," Jem pointed out. "If they wanted to hold someone hostage, wouldn't I be the ideal person?"

Max and Daniel exchanged glances.

"Don't treat me like I'm stupid. What are you not telling me?" Jem demanded.

"I think you should stay away from the club. Maybe we should get someone else to run it," Max admitted reluctantly.

Jem stared at him in horror. "For how long?"

"Forever. I think forever."

Griff

Griff wasn't stupid. He knew Jem had deliberately gotten rid of him. What he didn't know was why. Jem had seemed fine until they got in the car to return to the hospital. Then he'd gotten quieter and quieter, until Griff had given up trying to have a conversation with him. He was obviously worried about his brother. But maybe not. Maybe there was something Griff didn't understand.

When he reached the OR he saw a couple sobbing in each other's arms. For a moment he thought they were Pierre's parents until he spotted Mo returning with takeout cups. Mo grinned at him and then delivered the cups to another couple Griff hadn't spotted before. Mo had a quick word with them and then jogged over to Griff.

"I didn't expect to see you here. Where's your boy?"

"He was the one who sent me down here," Griff said. "How is the kid?"

"He's hanging on. That's all they keep telling us. They're doing tests at the moment, but then his parents will be allowed to visit him."

"Do you know what's going on?"

Mo should his head. "My orders are to make sure no one goes near Pierre or his parents."

"And who gave you the orders?"

Mo narrowed his eyes. "Am I missing something?"

"I think I am," Griff said ruefully. "My boy sent me away, and I don't know why."

Mo winced. "Okay, well, I got the orders from Quinn,

but he sounds very unhappy. There's big shit going down, Griff. That's why I'm surprised you're not by Jem's side."

"He's with Craig," Griff admitted. He wouldn't have confessed that to anyone except his fellow Daddies. "We had a session, which I thought would take his mind off the situation. And it did. But somewhere between the end of the session and coming back here, I've done something wrong. I just wish I knew what the hell it is."

"Then get back upstairs and sort it out, you idiot."

"Tactful as ever," Griff muttered.

Mo clapped an arm around Griff's shoulders. "You don't need tact. What you need is someone to tell you to put your ass in gear. Now get back upstairs and find out what's going on."

Griff chuckled although he didn't feel very humorous. But Mo was right. He needed to find out what was going on with his boy. "Thanks, Mo."

"You're welcome."

Griff narrowed his eyes. "Are you here on your own?"

"No, Lloyd and Doug are here. We're just keeping a very low profile."

"I really hope this kid survives," Griff admitted. "I don't think Jem will be able to deal with the guilt if he dies."

"Your boy takes too much on himself. I don't know what's going on, but I do know it's got nothing to do with him."

"He does take the weight of the world on his shoulders," Griff agreed.

He gave Mo a clap on the back and then headed back up to Max's room, feeling better for that brief discussion. Mo was a blunt man and always seem to put things in perspective.

As he left the elevator, he saw Craig and Quinn deep in

discussion, and then both of them turned to stare at him. That didn't look good. And where was Jem?

He joined them and went straight on the offensive. "Where's Jem?"

"He's in with his brother. It's not good, Griff. Max has gotten himself entangled in a nasty situation. He's probably going to go into witness protection," Quinn said in a low voice.

"Does Jem know this?" Griff demanded.

"I imagine he does now. He's been in there a long time, and I heard shouting." Craig gave him a wry smile.

"There's something else," Quinn said, and the serious look on his face made Griff's blood run cold.

"What is it?" He had to know. It had to do with him and Jem, he could tell that. But what had he done?

"Jem's asked that you no longer be on his protection detail. He doesn't want a Daddy."

Griff just stared at him. "What?"

Craig nodded unhappily. "I don't know what's happened, brother, but he's miserable."

"But—"

Quinn squeezed his shoulder. "Look, there's too much going on at the moment. Any other time, I'd leave you to deal with your boy. But until Max and probably also Pierre are in witness protection, I can't afford any distractions."

"You need to tell him the rest," Craig insisted.

Griff felt the anger start to burn inside of him and he had to take a deep breath not to let it all out. "Just spit it out."

"The cops think they could come after Jem next as he's Max's brother. They could try using him as leverage. They think Pierre was a warning, but Jem is even higher value."

"Then I need to get him away from here. I could take him up to Mo's cabin."

Quinn shook his head. "You're not taking him anywhere. I'm sorry, Griff, but this assignment is over. Take the rest of your vacation and come back after that. We'll find somewhere else for you to go."

"You're joking."

Quinn's expression was bleak. "I wish I were. But this is one arrangement that's come to an end. I'm sorry, but I need you to leave the hospital."

Griff was well trained enough to turn on his heel and stalk toward the elevator. Because if he didn't do that, he was going to take out his anger on two men who could easily beat him to a pulp. He didn't want to lose his job, but he had no idea what was happening. He couldn't leave his boy, not in the hands of people who didn't care about his needs. His phone pinged. He opened it up to see a message.

Jem is safe with me. I'll keep you informed. Craig

He knew that was meant to reassure him, but it had the opposite effect, making him more angry than ever. Craig had his own boy. He didn't need to be taking care of Griff's.

Griff stumbled out into the sunshine and glared up at the sun. He wasn't going home just to stare at the TV for hours until his vacation ended. He had to do something. He knew if he stayed at the hospital, Quinn and Craig would find out and he'd be escorted home. Where on earth were they going to hide Jem? He still wasn't allowed back at the club.

Griff had to sort this out and he knew only one person who could do that.

* * *

"I'm sorry, Griff. But we had to agree with his decision, until we know what the fuck is going on. He'll be safe, I promise you. Craig has agreed to take care of him." Dominic sighed as Griff paced around his office. "He's in good hands."

"The only hands he should be in are mine," Griff snapped.

"Until that can happen, he's being looked after. He is not your problem. Go home, finish your vacation, and wait for your new assignment."

Griff glowered at Dominic. "So that's it, is it? The client says fuck off, and I'm out of there? You didn't listen to any of the other clients when they said they didn't want a bodyguard."

Dominic ignored that comment. "Craig said Jem seemed upset, genuinely hurt. I haven't got time to pander to anyone's feelings now. Jem and Max are in danger. Let's place them somewhere safe and then we can deal with whatever is going on his head."

"He needs his Daddy," Griff snapped.

"His Daddy fucked up, and at the moment Jem's my client. Until that changes, his Daddy needs to get the fuck out of my office and go home."

Griff glowered at Dominic, but he knew when he was beaten. Dominic was the alpha dog of the alpha dogs. "What are you going to do with him?"

"He's gonna be offered the chance to go into witness protection with his brother."

"No!"

"You don't get a choice, Carlton."

Griff didn't reply. He wasn't going to incriminate himself. He left Dominic's office and headed for the double doors.

In the underground parking lot, Griff sat in his car and took a deep breath. Dominic had to be fucking insane if he thought he was gonna stay anywhere away from Jem. But first he needed to change vehicles.

Chapter Fifteen

Jem

People kept talking at him. Max was trying to persuade him to go into witness protection with him. Uncle Daniel kept talking about the legal implications. Jem knew he should be concerned about the club. Their heritage was at stake. Max and Daniel assured him that they could set up a company to run the club. There were plenty of experienced people who would jump at the chance of running a club like Peacock. But they weren't family. They didn't have the family link that he and Max had.

"We could go tonight," Max said. "CDR can pack our gear and we can be ready to go."

"Just like that?" Jem said faintly.

Max had been talking at him a mile a minute, but finally it seemed to get through that Jem was horrified by the idea. "We can start again, Jezza. A new life. A new chance. You know you've always said that you'd like to have the chance to try something new. The club was never your idea. I was the one who insisted we carry on with it."

That was true. Jem had still had dreams at that point of becoming a boy, but that had all been put on hold after their parents' death.

"I've given my life to that club," Jem said. "And now you're asking me to leave without thought?"

"You've got even fewer ties than I have."

Jem wanted to cry out, that wasn't true. He had a Daddy. But he didn't, because he'd sent Griff away. "I need to think. I need coffee."

He jumped to his feet and bolted from the room, almost colliding with Quinn, Craig, and Mo. There was no sign of Griff.

"Hey." Craig kept him on his feet. "Slow down."

Jem stared at him, his eyes wide. "They want to take me away."

Quinn gave him a curt nod, and Jem had the feeling he wasn't happy with him. "Yes, they want to put you into witness protection with your brother."

"I can't do that."

"You'll be able to live your lives without protection. You can start again somewhere."

"I can't..." He couldn't get the words out of his mouth, because he'd been the one to send Griff away. "There's got to be another way. Something else I can do."

He saw the three men exchange glances. "What?"

"We could put you into a safe house, but you still wouldn't be at the club, and who knows how long you'd have to be there? Witness protection is definitely the better idea."

"Unless you think you might miss someone," Craig suggested carefully. His eyes were fixed on Jem's face.

"I told him to leave," Jem whispered.

Suddenly there was only him and Craig in the hallway.

"He doesn't know why."

"He lied to me."

Craig furrowed his brow. "Griff never lies to anyone. None of us do."

"He talked to you and then told me everything was all right. But it wasn't, was it? My brother lied to me. First we nearly lost the club and now my whole world is going to shit. I can't deal with that, Craig, I can't deal with anybody lying to me."

"Were you a little when he had that conversation with me?"

Jem thought back. Then he nodded. He *had* still been in little space, but had then realized he couldn't be a little anymore.

"Griff wouldn't discuss anything adult with you when you are a little. It wouldn't be right," Craig suggested.

Jem pressed his lips together. He knew Craig was doing his best to reassure him, but Griff should have told him the truth. "I need coffee," he said, to get away. "I need to think."

"I'll come with you," Craig said.

Jem wanted to shriek at him that he could do this by himself, but he knew that he needed protection. He gave a curt nod and they headed toward the elevators.

"Where's Griff?" he asked.

"The last I heard he was shouting at Dominic," Craig said easily as he stabbed the button.

Jem winced. "About me?"

"You're the only thing he really shouts about."

There were too many people in the elevator for Jem to continue the conversation. In truth, he didn't know what to say. He still had issues about Griff not telling him the truth, even if his motives were good.

He followed Craig out of the elevator and to the café, still mulling on how he felt.

"Why didn't he stay?"

Craig didn't pretend not to know what he was talking about. Jem was grateful for that.

"Because Quinn ordered him out of the hospital, and Griff obeyed because he's that sort of guy."

"He's not a leader, he's the muscle."

Craig gave him an odd look. "Griff doesn't mind giving orders to his boys. But yes, he's got no desire to run a team at CDR. It's a shame, because he'd be good at it, but his interests lie elsewhere." The look he gave Jem made it clear exactly where his interests lay.

"But he could go to San Francisco and become a bodyguard there."

Now why had that just popped into his head? Jem remembered one of the first conversations at the club. Was it only two days ago? Griff had looked positively excited about the idea of going to San Francisco.

"I wonder what would happen to Doris?"

Craig chuckled. "Now I'm lost."

"Griff's dog, Doris. She gets looked after by a neighbor of his when he's at work. Who would look after her if Griff moved?"

"For someone who doesn't trust Griff, you sure are talking about him a lot."

Jem glowered at him. "I'm just musing."

"Let's worry about you first," Craig suggested.

Jem didn't want to think about himself. He didn't want to think about his situation at all. "I need coffee. Lots of coffee."

"I can do that," Craig assured him. He put a hand lightly at Jem's lower back, as if he didn't want to spook him. "It's been a stressful day for you."

Jem barked out a laugh. "That's one way of looking at it."

He felt a prickle between his shoulder blades and looked over his shoulder. He felt like somebody was watching him, but when he scanned the room, no one was paying him any attention. He kept a watchful eye as Craig paid for the drinks but, once again, no one was glancing his way.

Craig waited until he had a tray of coffees before he said to Jem, "You know Griff isn't your brother, don't you?"

"I know that," Jem muttered.

"Good, because I don't want you confusing the two of them. Griff is an honest man. Sometimes too honest."

"And you're saying Max isn't?" Jem asked sharply.

Craig said nothing.

Jem deflated. "I can't believe he did it again."

"An addiction is hard to break," Craig said. "Don't blame your brother for that. And this whole other mess, he must have been freaking out."

"Then why didn't he tell me?" Jem hissed.

"I don't know, Jem. I just know people make bad decisions when they're under stress."

Jem rolled his eyes at him. Could he be any less subtle?

Craig gave him a stern look. "I'd put my boy over my knees for being cheeky to me like that."

"It's a good thing I'm not your boy then." Although Jem had a feeling Griff would have done the same thing if he'd been here.

Back at Max's room, Mo took Max's and Daniel's coffee into them. Jem didn't feel like facing them yet.

Jem collapsed onto a couch and stared at his hands. "This morning I was worrying about Max dying, and now I'm worried about losing him for good. And now I face losing my life."

"Not your life," Quinn said. "This is to save your life."

Jem stared at him. "If this were you, what would you do?" Quinn hesitated and Jem nodded at him. "Precisely."

"You take after your uncle, boy," Mo said with a laugh.

Not your boy, Jem thought, but he was a boy. And if he went away he would lose that too. He was too old to find another community.

"What happens next?"

"Max is already in the system. US marshals are on their way to collect him." Quinn sat down next to him. "I know this is a really huge thing, Jem. But if Max stays here, he's in danger. I don't think his meeting with Pierre was by chance. I think Pierre was put here to keep an eye on him."

Jem stared at him, betrayed. "Pierre is a bad guy?" It sounded pathetic, but he couldn't process it.

"CDR have uncovered links between Pierre and the Mafia family. I'm sorry, Jem, but there's a good chance Pierre is the one who shot Max. Dominic called me while you were getting coffee with Craig."

Oh God, he needed Griff. He really needed Griff. What had he done, sending him away?

Griff

Griff knew Craig had made him, the second he walked into the café. He didn't expect anything less. He acknowledged Craig although he didn't give anything other than the merest nod. Craig was busy talking to Jem, who looked dreadful. Griff studied his boy, overwhelmed by the urge to rush over and find out what the problem was. Jem was white, and his eyes looked like dark shadows sunken in his face.

"You'd better be taking care of him," Griff muttered under his breath.

He had returned home, dressed in his leathers, and brought his Hog to the hospital. He would find it easier to follow on his bike, wherever they took Jem. He wouldn't let Jem out of his sight until he knew he was safe.

There was no way he was going to sit at home, watch TV, drink beer, and leave his boy to someone else... Griff tried to think of the end of that sentence, but all he could come up with was, he wasn't leaving his boy.

He didn't worry about Craig telling anyone he was there. Craig would have done the same thing for Louis. Griff hadn't sat in a club for weeks, only to walk away when his boy had a meltdown.

He watched them getting into the elevator. He was surprised when Jem looked over his shoulder a couple of times, but he didn't seem to see Griff who had retreated to the shadows. Did Jem sense he was here? It was a possibility.

The issue was when they were outside Max's room. He couldn't hang about without creating suspicion. Jem was with the three Biker Daddy Bodyguards, three men Griff trusted with his life. Griff decided to check out their exit strategies rather than risk being thrown out again.

He had paced around the hospital, planning four exit strategies, when someone tapped his shoulder. He looked round to see Jace grinning at him.

"Do you ever listen to Dominic?"

"No. Do you?"

"Not if I can help it."

Griff sighed. "I thought I was better trained than this."

"You are," Jace assured him. "Craig sent me a message to find you. He says Jem is going into witness protection. Whoa!" Jace grabbed Griff by the arms as Griff swayed. "Hey big guy, you need to get it together."

"He's doing what?" Griff hissed.

"He's going into witness protection with his brother. It's serious, Griff."

Griff shook his head. "No. He's not going anywhere without me. I don't care what happens to me, but I'm not leaving him."

Jace gave him a speculative look. "I don't know that you have much option in the matter. It's all arranged. They can't do anything until Max is discharged, but Jem is going to go with him."

Griff shook him off and folded his arms across his chest. "And whose idea was this? I'm damn sure Jem wouldn't have agreed to this."

"Jem loves his brother," a deep rumbling voice said behind him.

Griff wasn't surprised when he turned to find Quinn scowling at him. "He loves me too."

They hadn't gotten as far as that conversation yet, but Griff was supremely sure that Jem did love him.

"Jem's life is in danger."

"Then I'll look after him," Griff insisted.

Quinn's scowl deepened. "He's not going to leave his brother alone."

"Then we look after both of them."

"You're being ridiculous, Carlton. We don't have the resources to hide people. That's the US Marshal's job, not ours."

"We did with that British couple." Griff snapped his fingers, trying to remember what their name was.

The previous year, CDR had arranged protection for a gay British couple who had connections with Callum David Ross, the original founder of CDR. Griff hadn't met them, but he'd heard rumors that they were over here. If CDR could do it for one couple, they could do it for Jem, who had been a long-time client.

Quinn rolled his eyes. "You know no one is meant to know about that."

"Everybody knows about it," Griff pointed out.

"It was a favor to Cal Ross, and they crossed the Atlantic," Quinn said. "We haven't got the manpower to hide Jem and Max."

Griff pressed his lips together, holding back the angry words. They were prepared to look after strangers, but they wouldn't take care of one of their own. "Then I want to go into witness protection with him."

Quinn rocked back on his heels, and Griff saw the wide-eyed expression on Jace's face.

"You've got to be joking," Quinn exclaimed.

Griff shook his head. "He's my boy, and I'm not going to lose him now."

"You've only known him two days."

"How long did it take you to know that Cade was yours?" Griff demanded. "Or Craig and Louis, or Mo and Joseph?"

"He's got you there," Jace muttered from behind Quinn.

Quinn shook his head. "It's not the same."

"It is the same. I've known he was my boy from the minute I took him home from Romero. Do you think I spent night after night in a club because I like the music? Jem is mine, and I'm not letting him go."

"It's not your choice. Both Max and Jem have to agree."

Griff expelled a long breath. So Quinn would give way a little. If CDR wouldn't take care of Jem, then this was the next best thing. His family would be upset, but they would understand that he had to take care of Jem.

"You think they'd let me take Doris?"

"Yeah, I think they'd let you take that annoying mutt." Quinn grinned at Griff, but his expression was still grim. "Dominic's going to kill me."

"Yeah, I'm glad I'm not making that phone call." Griff wouldn't miss it for the world.

"Are you sure?" Quinn asked, his voice softening. "It's a huge step and I know what you mean about your boy, but it's still so new. What happens if it goes wrong? You could easily split up. And then you're left without your family and your friends. You barely know Jem Peacock, and now you're giving up your life for him."

"He's worth it," Griff murmured. "He's raw and untrained and so precious. He is an emerald in the rough and I want him to be by my side for the rest of my life. I'm not gonna let him go."

"I'm not happy about losing a Biker Daddy Bodyguard."

"I never really was one," Griff pointed out.

"Yeah, you were. The two months you spent sitting in the club proved that."

Griff stared at Quinn who just winked. "You mean that was a test?"

"No, that was you being all soppy over a boy. But it proved to us you had the tenacity to stay with a boy in need." Quinn shook his head again. "I didn't think I'd be losing you so quickly, though."

"If Max's case is resolved, then perhaps we could come back."

"Maybe," Quinn said noncommittally.

Craig and Mo were guarding Max's room.

"Don't tell me," Mo said to Quinn. "He's told you he's going with the boy."

"If you knew he was going to do that, you could have warned me," Quinn pointed out.

"I didn't think he'd be that stupid."

Griff flipped them all off. "Nothing is arranged yet. Let me talk to the brothers before you all start writing me off."

Craig clapped him on the back. "He needs you, brother."

"I wish we could have had a play date with Louis first." Griff was quite regretful about that. It would have been good for Jem.

"Louis would have liked that," Craig agreed.

* * *

Jem sat next to Max, who appeared to be sleeping. Jem looked miserable, and it wasn't hard to see that he'd been crying, his cheeks still wet from tears. He didn't bother to look over as Quinn and Griff walked into the room.

"You've got a visitor," Quinn said.

Jem turned and his expression went from miserable to joyful and relieved, to a bleakness Griff never wanted to see again. "I told you that Griff is not my bodyguard anymore."

Griff went to answer but Quinn nudged him, and he subsided.

"Yeah, try telling him that," Quinn drawled. "Anyway, things have moved on since then."

"What do you mean?" Jem asked suspiciously.

"Griff has asked to be put into witness protection with you."

Jem's jaw dropped open. He stared at Griff. It was hard to miss the relief and joy in his eyes. "You want to come with me? Are you insane?" he spluttered.

Griff went over to Jem and pulled him into his arms. Then he spoke in Jem's ear, the conversation for Jem alone. "I would follow you to the ends of the earth, Jem Peacock. I can't imagine life without you. You are my boy, and I want you to be my lover. The question is, will you say yes?"

Chapter Sixteen

Jem

Jem shivered in Griff's arms. Griff was holding him so tight he could barely breathe, yet it wasn't tight enough. He wanted to be absorbed into Griff's embrace and never have to move again.

"You can't give up your life for me," he muttered.

"I'm not giving up my life for you," Griff said. "I'm starting it. With my boy."

Jem pulled back to look into Griff's eyes, seeking any doubt there. But there was nothing but confidence. He opened his mouth, but Griff put a finger over his lips.

"If you're going to ask me if I'm sure one more time, I am."

Jem shut his mouth. Griff bent to kiss his lips.

"Great, I'm going to have to spend all my time watching you two drooling over each other," Max said, but he didn't sound upset, more resigned.

The other Daddies were huddled by the door of the

room, smug looks on their faces. Jem knew Griff was going to get a lot of grief for this, at least while he was here.

"What about Doris?" Jem murmured.

"She's coming with us. I don't think I could leave her here, not even with Rob."

Jem breathed a sigh of relief. He knew Griff would have struggled to leave his beloved dog behind.

Jem looked at Max. "We'll need to talk about the club. Whether we shut it down or keep it running with a different management team."

"Elise would be a very good manager," Max said. He yawned, and grimaced. "I need to sleep."

The high color was back in his cheeks. He still hadn't gotten over the infection.

"We can leave you alone. You're not ready to move yet," Quinn said. He looked at Griff. "Can we talk to you and Jem outside please?"

Griff looked at Jem. Jem nodded and bent to kiss Max on the forehead.

"I'll be back in a minute."

Max wrapped his hand around Jem's forearm. "Wait."

"I'll be outside," Griff said, and left the room.

As the door closed, Max gave Jem a tired smile. "Thanks for coming with me. It would have been so hard to be on my own."

Jem patted his hand. "You're my family. Of course I'd come with you."

Max was snoring before Jem had left the room, a slight smile on his face.

An additional man joined the CDR men. Jem had met Dominic Cook when CDR took over security for the club. Jem was more worried about the way Griff was frowning.

Jem went over to him. "Is something wrong?"

"Dominic has another suggestion, but I told him it's not my decision. It must be something you and Max agree together."

Jem snuggled into Griff who hugged him, and then he looked at Dominic. "What do you suggest?"

Dominic glowered at him, his dark brows knitted together. Under normal circumstances Jem would have quailed, but he had his Daddy beside him and, from the looks on the CDR men's faces, this was a normal expression for Dominic.

"Quinn told me that he'd already talked to Griff about setting up a Biker Daddy Bodyguards elsewhere. How do you feel about moving with us, rather than going into witness protection? We have other plans in mind."

Jem furrowed his brow. "You want us to move to San Francisco?"

"I want you to move to London."

Griff choked. "London? What the hell?"

"Josh Cooper and Liam Quick have talked about this for a while. They've asked for someone to go over and train up their guys. I can't afford to let Quinn or Craig go for any length of time, and Mo needs to stay with Joseph. But if you and Griff have to leave, then why not go somewhere where you're needed?"

"Max?"

"He's going with you. We're going to move him tonight to somewhere safe. You'll have medical help."

Griff bent down to whisper in Jem's ear. "It would be a new start for all of us."

"But London?" Jem had done little traveling because of the club, and London seemed a lifetime away.

Craig came over and looked at Griff for permission before he took one of Jem's hands in his. "If you come over to London, you'd still see Cade and Louis, and hopefully Joseph. You won't lose track of your previous life."

"But what will I do over there?" Jem said.

Griff's smile was reassuring. "You and Max have mad skills. I'm sure you'll think of something."

Jem's head was spinning just at the thought of moving half a world away. "What about going into witness protection?"

"Leave that with me. I've already spoken to Deputy US Marshal Colm Riordan. He shouted, I shouted back. All is good," Dominic said.

"Who is Colm Riordan?" Jem muttered to Griff.

"Absolutely no idea," Griff whispered. "Just leave it with Dominic."

"I haven't got a passport," Jem said. "I've not had a chance to go anywhere for years."

Dominic nodded. "We can sort that out. All I need from you is the go-ahead to get this organized. We can arrange a protection detail until you're ready to go."

Jem looked up at Griff. "What do you think?"

In his mind he added the Daddy on the end, and from Griff's expression, he heard the unspoken word.

"I'd rather be with you, surrounded by my friends, than be with you on my own. I'll go into witness protection with you, but this seems a good way to get far away from the issues Max is facing, and start a new life."

"What about his gambling?" Jem quailed at the thought of trying to cope with his brother's addiction somewhere new.

"We can deal with that over there," Craig said. "Liam has already arranged counseling for him."

Jem wanted to cry at how kind people were in the most traumatic moments of his life. He laid his head on Griff's shoulder and let Griff hug him, while he said the words that would change his and Max's life forever.

"Let's go to London."

He just hoped Max would forgive him.

* * *

Jem curled up with Doris on the couch, scratching behind her ears as the dog rumbled happily. He sucked on his purple binky and cuddled Bridget in the other arm.

Griff was in the next apartment talking to Rob about his sudden move, although he wasn't saying where. Rob had agreed to hold onto Doris until they could arrange to get her vaccination passport and move her. Griff had introduced Rob to Craig, and they were making the arrangements between them. Rob was sad that he wouldn't be seeing Doris again, although he confessed he'd been looking at shelters to get a dog of his own. Griff told Jem he would happily pay any adoption fees as thanks for all the help Rob had given him. Jem felt rather sorry for Rob as he was going to lose Griff and Doris. Jem had an inkling that Rob had a crush on Griff, although Griff had never noticed. Jem was suddenly fiercely glad that he didn't have to fight the next-door neighbor for Griff's attention. His Daddy was all his. Griff had agreed to sublet his apartment to one of the Daddies in the community, and Rob had perked up at the idea of another hot gay guy moving in next door.

Griff's family was another matter, and Jem knew Griff was more upset than he pretended to be about losing his family. Quinn had promised to look out for them, and they would be able to see him in London, which was more than they could do if he was in witness protection.

Peacock was another matter. That was going to take

longer to deal with. There had been a tentative approach to Elise with the idea of becoming the manager of Peacock. So far it looked promising, and Louis had promised to keep an eye on the place as part of his expanding empire. Jem wondered if Max would prefer in the end to sell to Louis. But that was a conversation for another day. Max was in a safe house and CDR were arranging for his removal to London.

Jem was where he wanted to be. With his Daddy. Or he would be when he came back from his hot next-door neighbor. Jem frowned.

"What's the matter, baby boy?" His Daddy sat down next to him, careful not to disturb Doris.

"You were long time," Jemmy grumbled.

"I'm sorry," his Daddy apologized. "There was a lot to talk about. Did Doris look after you?"

Doris rumbled happily at the sound of her name.

"Jemmy wants playtime," Jemmy said.

His Daddy cupped his head, entangling his fingers in his hair. "We can do that."

Jemmy chewed on his lip.

"Baby boy?"

"I need my diapy changed," he whispered.

"We can do that too."

Griff scooped Jem off the couch as if he barely weighed a thing. He carried him down to the playroom and into the closet to lay him on the changing mat.

"What if they come in?" Jemmy said.

Two of the CDR men were guarding the door, but Jemmy didn't know them.

"They won't come in without warning," Griff promised. "It's just Daddy and his baby boy tonight."

"Promise."

"I promise, Jemmy," Griff said as he unfastened the diaper. "It's just you and me."

Jem sighed as Griff cleaned him gently. "I like that."

Griff

Griff packed up the playroom as Jemmy had a tea party with all the dolls. It didn't take long as most of the toys were in boxes already. Movers were coming to pack up his apartment for their trip to London the next day, but there were certain items Griff didn't want the movers to see and they were in a suitcase ready to go with Jem and Griff.

Jem would take his dolly and his pacifier with him, and Griff had packed a few other items so that they were able to play when they arrived in London.

But for now, he had the chance to watch Jem relax and play with the dollies. He had ignored most of the cars and the trains.

"Jemmy, shall we give Daddy Mo the cars and the trains so that Joseph can play with them?"

Jemmy looked over at Griff, a bright smile on his face. "Yes, Daddy. That would be a good thing to do. That would be sharing."

Jemmy went back to his game as Griff sent a message. He received a response about five minutes later.

Groan. I can't walk around here without tripping over trains. He would love more.

Joseph was a billionaire businessman and could afford more trains than Griff could imagine, but he loved playing with other boy's train sets. Jemmy was right. It was a good thing to do.

It was also one less thing to take with him. He put the boxes of trains and cars aside for Mo and Joseph. If

Jemmy changed his mind, they could get more toys in London.

It was their last night together before they left Seattle. Jem's and Max's apartments had already been emptied and were in storage. Griff's was the last one. Max had flown on ahead, being the biggest security risk, with CDR men guarding him. He would be met at the other end by men from their liaison security company, QuickFire, ready to take over.

Doris had moved in with Rob in the short term, but she would be ready to leave soon. Which left Griff and Jemmy. Dominic wanted them to leave as soon as possible. There had been chatter about a bounty on Jem's head. They were taking flights in the morning.

Griff wasn't sure how he felt about the impending move. He had been so busy he had stopped thinking about it, but now it caught up with him. He sat down suddenly and stared at his hands. Then Jemmy crawled over to him and scrambled up into his lap.

"What's wrong, Daddy?" He looked worried as he cupped Griff's jaw.

"I think it just hit me what we're doing," Griff confessed. "Don't worry, it's not that I don't want to go. It's just that I've been so busy organizing everything that I haven't had a chance to think about it."

Jemmy kissed Griff on the cheek and then on the other cheek. "I've had too much time to think about it," he admitted. "If it hadn't been for this—" he pointed at the toys, "—I think I might have freaked out more."

Griff clutched Jemmy to his heart. "You have been the most amazing boy in the world. I love you."

"I love you, Daddy." Jemmy buried his face in the crook of Griff's neck. His cheeks were warm against Griff's skin.

"Jemmy, can I take you to bed?"

"I thought you were never going to ask."

They hadn't done much more than play since the decision to leave for London was made. There had been one or two blow jobs, but that had been more about relieving frustration than sexual desire. They had been so busy talking and thinking and planning, that taking their relationship further had vanished out of the window.

Griff felt Jemmy rock against him. "Baby boy?"

He slid his hand down between the two of them to palm against the hard shaft in Jemmy's onesie. Jemmy moaned into Griff's skin.

He wasn't wearing a diaper. He didn't always when they played. Griff left it to him to decide what he was comfortable doing. So there was just a thin layer of cotton between him and Griff's hand. Griff wrapped the cotton and his hand around Jemmy's dick.

"You feel so good," Griff murmured.

Jemmy slid his hand into Griff's sweatpants. They had both had a bath, so Griff hadn't bothered with briefs. Jemmy wrapped his hand around Griff's cock. Griff wanted to thrust up hard into Jemmy's hand.

"Can we take this to bed?" Jemmy begged.

Without another word Griff got to his feet and carried Jemmy to their bedroom, tripping on a suitcase so that they both crashed to the bed, but Griff managed to avoid falling on top of Jem. Somewhere between the playroom and the bedroom Jemmy had become Jem again.

Jem was frantic, his hands running all over Griff's torso and back, cupping his ass and thrusting against his groin. Griff raised his head to look down into the emerald-green eyes.

"Are you sure you want to do this?"

Jem's dark eyebrows met over his nose. "More than sure."

"If I scare you. If there's anything that scares you, I will stop, I promise you." Griff really needed Jem to know that. He wouldn't frighten his boy for the world. He was not that kind of man.

"You don't scare me," Jem said.

Griff smiled down at him, reassured, and brushed his lips over Jem's mouth. Jem parted his lips and Griff thrust his tongue in. Jem's tongue slid against his and they dueled together in a lazy dance.

Griff cupped Jem's face with his hands as he focused all his attention on Jem's mouth. Jem kissed him back just as eagerly. They stayed where they were, kissing, until Griff had to pull back, his lungs burning.

"I need to feel your skin," he said.

He wriggled back so he could unsnap the onesie, and he peeled it down Jem's lithe body. Usually Jem let him, but this time he wriggled so that Griff would get on with it. Jem's gaze was fixed on him, as Griff pulled the T-shirt over his head.

"One day I'm going to lick every line of your ink," Jem promised.

Griff shivered at the thought. "When we're in London I'm going to get extra ink to celebrate finding my boy."

Jem moaned, letting Griff know he loved the idea.

"Do you have any tattoos?" Griff hadn't seen them, but he could have missed a small one.

Jem shook his head. "I never met anybody that was worth it."

His expression told Griff exactly what he meant. His Daddy was worth it.

Griff wriggled out of his sweatpants, and then he was

naked over Jem, spreading out so their erections rubbed each other with delicious friction, pre-come licking over their bellies. He could feel the hairs on their legs tangle together, and smell the musk arising from Jem. They were one, they were together.

Jem's skin was pale compared to his, his nipples dusky pink compared to Griff's copper color. Griff couldn't stop staring at the two of them together.

"I need you inside me," Jem whispered.

"I want to fill you up and mark you as mine," Griff muttered. Yeah, he was a possessive bastard.

"I haven't...for a long time," Jem said.

"We'll go slowly," Griff promised. "It's been a while for me too."

He reached over to the nightstand and pulled out foil packets and lube.

"I wanted to get tested. I want you to be bare inside me," Jem said fiercely.

"We'll do that as soon as we get to London," Griff promised. The thought of filling up his boy with his seed made it even harder to keep his control.

He squeezed lube on his fingers and rolled so that he could slide a finger between Jem's ass cheeks. Jem pulled his knees back to his chest and Griff nearly lost his fragile control at the sight of the pink hole flexing and waiting for him.

"Come on," Jem urged.

Griff pressed one finger in, taking his time until Jem was relaxed, then two, seeking out the sweet pleasure spot that would make Jem buck up and cry out. He smiled when he found it. Jem grabbed Griff's biceps, his nails digging in.

"I need more," he begged. "So much more."

By the time Griff had slid three fingers inside and

prepared him, Jem was a crying mess. Griff raised up to lean over Jem, and kissed his mouth.

"The next time we do this, we'll be half a world away."

He pressed in and Jem gasped, spreading his legs wider, trying to force Griff inside. Griff took his time, but Jem didn't want that.

"More," he demanded. He pulled Griff against him until Griff was balls deep inside.

Griff scowled down at his boy. "I'm sorry, my boy. Who do you think is in charge?"

Jem's eyes opened wide. "You, Daddy. Only you."

"Then why did you pull me against you?"

"I needed you inside me." Jem bit his bottom lip. "I'm sorry, Daddy."

Griff's expression softened and he pushed back the damp hair from Jem's face. "I don't want to hurt you, baby boy."

"You never hurt me," Jem whispered. "But thank you for taking care of me."

"Always," Griff promised. "But for being impatient, I decide when you can come."

"Yes, Daddy."

Griff was sure that was a smug smirk playing on Jem's lips. So his boy did have a naughty side. Well, Jem would discover what it was like to be brought to the brink of climax over and over but not be allowed to come. Griff gave Jem a wicked smile and saw his boy's sudden wary expression.

"Don't worry, my boy. I'll let you come—eventually."

Jem whimpered.

Chapter Seventeen
6 months later – south London

Jem

Jemmy swallowed nervously at the knock at their front door. Doris looked up, excitement in her eyes.

Griff held up his hand for Jemmy to wait. Jemmy nodded.

"Doris, Doris, Doris?"

Jemmy winced. He may have perfect pitch, but Cade was really loud. There would be another complaint from their elderly neighbor. She complained every time Max did it. Yes, Max the dog hater had turned into Doris's biggest fan. He kept threatening to kidnap her.

"She's going to kill us," Griff muttered as he went to the front door.

Doris lifted up her head.

"Doris, Doris, Doris?"

Ohooooooooooooooooooooo!

Doris galloped down the hall as Griff opened the front door.

"Oof. Jesus, Doris, you're built like a tank." Craig staggered back under the weight of the dog, who was determined to love him. Behind him his boy snickered loudly. Craig scowled at Louis who just raised one eyebrow.

"You were the one determined to greet the dog first of all, it's your own fault."

"Doris, I had a shower this morning, you don't have to lick my entire face. Griff, what do you feed this dog? Her breath stinks."

The rest of the men ignored Craig's complaints as they shuffled into the hallway, hugging Griff as they passed him. They had agreed that until they reached the main room, there was no difference between the Daddies and the boys.

Jemmy watched from the doorway, butterflies in his stomach. What if they laughed at him? He wore his favorite dress, with yellow flowers and his ankle socks had a yellow lace trim. He knew the Daddies and boys were expecting it, but being told and seeing it for themselves was another matter. But the three boys rushed toward him and he found himself enfolded in Louis's strong arms.

"I love your dress," Louis said when he let Jemmy go. He traced the pattern on the dress. "The flowers are so pretty." He sounded almost envious.

Then he was passed to Joseph who hugged him tight and kissed him on the cheek. "Thank you for the train set. My daddy complained a lot that there were more trains, but he likes playing with them just as much as I do. And all those cars were good. I brought one of them with me. Look." He held out a blue car that had apparently come from Griff's set.

Jemmy gave him a nervous smile. Joseph talked so fast he could barely understand him, but he was glad the cars and trains had made him happy.

Then Cade was in front of him. He'd met Cade once or

twice at Peacock, but he hadn't had time to develop as much of a relationship with him as he had with the others, because Cade was always working.

"Thank you to you and Daddy Griff for inviting us," Cade said in a rush as though he'd been told to say it. "I like your dress."

Then the three boys were in the main room crying out in excitement at the toys that were laid out for them to play with. Jemmy looked up to see the four Daddies staring at him. He sought out his Daddy for reassurance. Griff nodded his head in encouragement.

Daddy Mo, who was the oldest, and in Jem's mind the scariest, looked at Griff for permission. Griff nodded. then Daddy Mo walked down the hall and knelt in front of Jemmy.

"It's good to see you, Jemmy. You look very pretty. You tell me if Joseph doesn't share, okay?"

"I will," Jemmy promised as Daddy Mo gave him a hug.

Both Daddy Quinn and Daddy Craig asked permission from his Daddy to hug him. Griff had already asked him earlier in the day if that was okay. Griff was like that. He was always negotiating with Jem, even if Jemmy would prefer he didn't.

But the hugs from Daddy Quinn and Daddy Craig were good, and then everyone was in the main room. His Daddy closed the door, and the outside world was shut out. It was just Daddies and their littles.

This was the first time they'd seen their friends from Seattle since they'd arrived in London. Cade and his band, Daysance, were over for interviews for their new album.

His Daddy frowned. "Isn't Ian coming? I thought you were taking care of him, Quinn."

"He's gone to pick up Graham from the airport. They'll be here later," Quinn said.

The former Granddaddy of the Seattle Daddy community and his young boy were also in London. It was the first time Graham had been here, and his boy was looking forward to showing him around. Jemmy didn't expect to see much of them, as Ian was so excited to see his Daddy again.

The afternoon went as expected, with Cade and Joseph playing with the cars and trains, and Louis whispering with Jemmy in the corner. Jemmy had made friends in London, but it was such a relief to talk to people he knew from Seattle. And it turned out Louis liked playing with the dolls as much as Jemmy did.

Louis smoothed down the red velvet on a doll's cape. "So how are you really doing?"

Jemmy scowled at him, not liking his little space broken.

"Louis, what did I tell you about waiting to ask Jemmy all the questions later?" Daddy Craig scolded.

Louis hung his head. "I'm sorry, Jemmy."

Jemmy reached over and hugged Louis, whispering in his ear, "I'm good. This is the right place for us to be."

Louis hugged him back. "I was worried. The guys here are wonderful, but it's not like being at home."

"At least no one wants to kill us here," Jemmy said.

Louis chuckled and then, at another scowl from his Daddy, he subsided, and they went back to playing with the dolls.

When they got tired, all the boys sat with their Daddies while they ate cookies and drank milk. Doris snuffled around, hoping one of the boys would give in and feed her a cookie. Their visitors were suffering from jetlag, and Jemmy swore Mo and Quinn napped for a bit while Craig talked to Griff. Jemmy climbed into his Daddy's lap because he was tired and ready for a nap. He caught Louis's wistful gaze. Louis was larger and heavier than his Daddy, and he'd once confided in Jem that he wished he'd been born a twink.

"Rather than a gorgeous, handsome man who has all the men drooling." Jem had added the last part, and Louis laughed at him, but the wistfulness was real. Craig patted the seat beside him, and Louis sat down, Craig's arms around him in an instant, kissing the top of his head. It was clear Craig thought his boy was perfect.

Jemmy half-listened to the conversation between Griff and Craig. Most of it was shoptalk about CDR and the bodyguards. Jemmy wasn't much interested. But then he heard Max's name mentioned and he listened more closely. Max had been invited for the afternoon, but he'd declined, saying they would be more comfortable without him, which was true, but it had been very nice, and out of character for him to be that thoughtful. What was Craig about to tell his Daddy?

Griff

Griff knew how worried Jemmy had been about the whole day, but everyone had treated him with the greatest respect. Even Joseph, who had been way more interested in the cars and the trains than what Jemmy was wearing. Griff hadn't worried about the Daddies. They were the most non-judgmental people he'd ever met. And it was good to catch up with them.

Like Jemmy, he enjoyed London more than he thought he would. Josh Cooper drove him insane, although the man was a freaking genius when it came to intel. Thankfully, Griff's actual boss, Liam Quick, was a good balance against Josh's insanity. But it wasn't the same as working for CDR.

After a while, Mo and Quinn fell asleep, which left Craig rolling his eyes, but he caught Griff up with all the gossip.

"It turns out I discovered what Detective Hamilton had against Jem and Max," Craig said with a grin.

Griff furrowed his brow. "You did?" He'd never managed to work out what the detective's grievance was.

Craig smirked at him. "Elise is a mine of information. You should have asked her. Would you believe it was because he'd been turned down for membership of Peacock?"

Griff's jaw dropped open. "He was going to get Jem jailed for murder because he didn't get membership of the club?"

"Yep. She found out from the female detective who was his new partner. She doesn't have much time for him, but she did tell Elise he was a good detective. Usually. She and Elise are..." Craig didn't need to finish the sentence.

Griff grunted. "*Was* his new partner? Past tense?"

"She threw chai latte over him. The partnership didn't last."

The detective had been about to put his boy in jail. He deserved more than a coffee shower.

He stroked Jemmy's hair, loving the soft feel of it under his palm. Jemmy was warm in his arms and he loved being able to hold him in front of all his friends.

Craig grinned at him as if he'd sympathized with Griff's feelings about Hamilton. "We have some good news about Max."

Griff felt the sudden tension through Jemmy, and he held him tighter, knowing Jem was suddenly awake. He felt sad, hoping that his little boy would return later. "Don't keep me waiting."

He saw Craig's eyes flicker to Jem and he nodded.

"The threat to Max's life has been removed. Permanently."

"Seriously?"

Craig's smile was huge. "There was turf warfare between factions of the mob. The people who were after Max are no longer a threat, shall we say. We've had it on good authority that no one is interested in Max or what he saw."

Griff expelled a long breath. "That's good to hear." He felt Jem shaking in his arms and held him tighter. "Does Max know?"

"Dominic is going to call him this afternoon. You can come home if you want to."

Griff felt strangely reluctant, although if Jem wanted to return home he would. He'd found it easier to settle than Jem had, because setting up a new Biker Daddy Bodyguards kept him occupied. "I feel like we've only just gotten here."

"I wouldn't rush back. The chance to work in another country for a while? I think you'd be an idiot to return home. I just have to persuade my boy to do more traveling. He's promised me we can go back to Paris soon."

"It's not just my decision," Griff said. "My boy gets to decide too."

"I heard he and Max were thinking of opening up a new club?"

"They are. But not like Peacock. It's a club for people like us."

"Max is willing to open a club like that? I thought he was all designer suits and people with large wallets."

"I think Max has hidden depths that haven't been plumbed yet," Griff said diplomatically. He smirked as he felt, rather than heard, Jem's snort. Craig returned his smirk. "Also he's met some boys with large wallets."

Max and Jem had had many discussions about their new club. They had discussed the potential of opening separate venues, but finally admitted to each other that they liked working together. So Little Peacock would take planning, but it was in the works.

When everybody had left, Jem was back in his onesie as he cleared away the toys in the main room. Griff took Doris around the block for a walk and returned to find Jem on the couch cuddling Bridget and sucking furiously on his binky. Which meant his boy was thinking hard.

"We can go home," he said to Jem as he sat on the couch.

"Is that what you want?" Jem frowned, looking very worried.

"Don't you?" Griff countered.

Jem looked out of the window, at the lights of the cars passing with monotonous regularity. "I don't know. I like it here."

Griff drew his boy into his arms. "You heard what I said to Craig?"

Jem nodded. "I did. Thank you for including me in the decision."

"I promised you I'd do that."

"I called Max while you were out. He'd already heard from Dominic."

"What does he think?" Griff asked.

"He doesn't want to go home. He likes it here. It turns out he's met somebody."

Griff said nothing, as he'd already discovered that on the grapevine.

Jem smacked him in the shoulder. "You already knew that, didn't you?"

"Ouch! You're not meant to beat up your Daddy. But yes, I did know. Max isn't very subtle, and I was worried about the changes in his routine. I think we should get him round here to talk about it."

"His new relationship?"

Griff rolled his eyes at him. "No, going home to Seattle. He can't make a life-changing decision on the basis of meeting somebody."

"You did," Jem said pointedly.

"Touché." His boy knew where to stab him.

"You're right, though, we do need to talk to him. But what about you? You're the one setting up a new organization here. Max and I haven't even started yet."

Griff thought about it for a long while as Jem cuddled in his arms. "I think we have a brand-new opportunity, and I think we should give it everything we've got."

"Won't you miss your friends?"

"Yes, but they'll come here. Quinn said if he didn't travel with Cade, he'd never get to see him. And you know how big Daysance is over here."

"It sounds as if the three of us are staying in London," Jem murmured.

Griff bent to kiss Jem's lips, loving the way Jem melted into his arms. "Welcome to our new world, my boy."

THE END

From Sue Brown:

Do you like to walk on the darker side of romance? Then click here for the first book in the spin-off series, Dark Heart. I decided to take a darker turn with the spin-off,

Darker Daddy Bodyguards. There are familiar faces but it's whole lot more dangerous with my Mafia Daddies.

A teaser from the first book, Dark Heart.

Leon

The four black-clad men spread out, snow crunching under their boots, seemingly poised to strike. One of the guys could make two of Leon, width, and height. The others were shorter and leaner.

Leon tucked Nico behind him, shielding him with his larger body. If they came for his boy, they'd have to go through him. He'd die but he'd sure as hell kill as many as he could first.

"Stay behind me," he ordered Nico.

"We're fucked," Nico hissed.

His boy's assessment of the situation was remarkably astute. They were totally fucked.

He wished he'd listened to Ryder.

The sound of Leon's cell ringing at dark-thirty was unwelcome. The information even more so.

"Trasker. You're gonna be offered an assignment. Don't take the call."

Leon blinked at Quinn Ryder's clipped tone. His first reaction was to tell him to fuck off. No one told Leon what assignment to take. Not even a man he'd called friend for nearly twenty years.

"Why?" he demanded.

"You won't make it out alive."

"Like I haven't heard that before," Leon scoffed.

"This comes from Cooper."

Leon grunted. He knew Josh Cooper. Short, blond,

annoying, and with the sharpest brain in the business. "I'll think about it."

"Live or die. It's up to you."

Then Ryder was gone, and Leon flopped back onto his pillows and closed his eyes.

Nice!

Dammit, he was on vacation anyway. He'd ignored every call offering him work. The previous assignment had left him with a bullet through his left bicep and he was lucky to still have full use of his arm. He was back to fitness, but he needed a break. It wasn't only the physical effects of being shot he needed to get over.

Leon opened his eyes and squinted at his phone long enough to switch it off. Now no one could get hold of him. He threw his phone on the nightstand and snuggled under the covers. This bodyguard was unavailable for hire.

The knock at the door should have warned him. Leon was having a late breakfast, sitting on the couch watching daytime TV. He crammed his sandwich in his mouth as he checked his phone to see who stood outside his front door. He wasn't surprised to see his sister looking up at the camera, making rude gestures. Leon received two people to his door. Marilyn and the pizza guy. On balance he preferred the pizza guy.

Leon opened the door and grinned at his sister. "What do ya want?"

Then he saw two things. Her frightened expression and the man who stood two feet away pointing a Beretta at her.

Leon's Glock was stowed, but his Ruger was in his ankle holster. Even on vacation he was strapped. But Leon knew if he went for it both he and his sister would be dead before he reached it. He ignored the man, focusing his whole atten-tion on his sister. "Marilyn?"

She grabbed at his hands, holding him with a fierce grip. "I'm sorry, Leon. They grabbed me as I dropped Noah at school."

"Where's Noah?" Leon snapped, flames exploding in his head as he thought of his five-year-old nephew being kidnapped or worse.

"Noah is fine, Mr. Trasker," the man said, his accent smooth, hard to place.

He was younger than Leon, black-clad in a designer suit Leon recognized. He had the same suit in his wardrobe. He had large, deep brown eyes, and thick lashes, and his wavy dark hair smoothed back from his handsome, tanned face. Leon might have liked him under different circumstances, but he had a Beretta pointed at Marilyn. He was a dead man walking as far as Leon was concerned.

The man smiled. Leon didn't return the smile.

"Where is he?" he demanded.

"He's with his teacher, Mrs. Shaw. We're not interested in hurting a *bambino*. We only want to talk to you."

"Then why didn't you call me?" Leon snapped. "Instead of kidnapping and scaring the living crap outta my sister."

"We tried," the man murmured. "It kept going to voicemail."

Crap. He'd forgotten to switch his phone on after Quinn Ryder's call.

"We need to come in, Mr. Trasker."

Leon eased his sister into the apartment, the man following still aiming his weapon at Marilyn's back. He was following by two other men, one a man mountain and the other shorter and leaner, with flat, cold expression.

"Let my sister go," Leon ordered.

"I'm afraid I can't do that, Mr. Trasker. Not until you agree to come with me."

"And if I don't come with you?"

The guy shrugged. "Ms. Trasker is my surety of your good behavior."

"Do as he asks, Leon," Marilyn begged, now clutching at his arm, her grip so tight it was painful, and her blue eyes wide and frightened. "They said they'll kill Noah if you don't go with them."

"I won't let them touch you or Noah," Leon promised, his gazed fixed on her. "No one hurts Noah."

"I knew you were a sensible man," the man said.

Leon glared at him. "Who are you?"

"Gianni Acierno," the man said without hesitation.

"What do you want with me? I have nothing to do with your family."

Leon knew who the Acierno family were. Anyone who lived in Seattle did. But he was a professional bodyguard. He'd stayed well away from mafia gangs, mobs, and cartels, and intended to keep it that way.

"You come with a reputation," Acierno said. "We need you."

Leon knew what that reputation was, but it wasn't something he wanted to discuss in front of his sister. "You've got your own muscle. Why me?"

Acierno hesitated. Leon noticed it. Leon generally ignored what came out of people's mouths. People lied. It was their body language that he paid attention to. Folks didn't know what they gave away. The hesitation told him Acierno didn't know why Leon was needed and wasn't happy about it.

Then Acierno said, "You get the job done whatever the cost."

Leon had heard that one before.

Marilyn looked between them and frowned. "What's he talking about, Leon? What did you do?"

"My job," Leon said shortly. "Like I always do. Kidnapping my sister at gunpoint and threatening my nephew's life is not how I agree to do business."

"We needed to get your attention," Acierno said smoothly, his uncertainty gone, leaving behind the threat that if Leon didn't obey, Marilyn would pay a high price.

"You've got it. Now let Marilyn go home."

Acierno nodded and two of the huge musclemen took a step in their direction. Marilyn whimpered and threw herself against Leon who put her behind him, shielding her from the goons.

Leon scowled at them. "Touch my sister again and it'll be the last thing you do," he warned. "I'll drive her home and then I'll come with you."

"No!" Marilyn clung onto Leon's hoodie. "You can't leave me there alone."

"We'll drive you both back to her home." Leon opened his mouth to protest but Acierno shook his head. "It's non-negotiable."

Leon turned to look at Marilyn. "You can go stay with Frank and Jenny. They can take you to collect Noah this afternoon."

Marilyn's next-door neighbors were two retired homicide cops. Leon had checked them both out when Marilyn moved into the house. Frank was old-school. Shoot first, ask questions later. Jenny was the scariest cop Leon had ever met. His sister would be safe with them.

Marilyn nodded. He could see she was hanging onto her self-control by a thread. Leon cupped her face and smiled at her.

"You and Noah are gonna be fine, Maz."

"And what about you?" she whispered, her blue eyes filling with tears as she wrapped her hands around his wrists.

"I'll be fine too," he promised. "This is business. I'll go talk to old man Acierno."

Out of the corner of his eye, he caught Gianni Acierno's immediate scowl and pursed lips at the perceived disrespect to the Don. Poking the tiger when he was holding a gun on you was a stupid move. Leon could live with it. In this space, he was the tiger too.

"I need to change," he said.

Acierno gave a swift nod to the larger of the goons who stalked over to Leon. Marilyn shrank back and whimpered as Leon made her sit on the couch where he'd been before the knock at his door.

"I'll be five minutes. They won't hurt you," Leon promised.

Acierno inclined his head. "We don't want to hurt you, ma'am, as long as your brother cooperates."

They had Leon by the throat, and he and they knew it. There were only two people in the world he cared about: his sister and his nephew. The Aciernos would pay for threatening his family. He nodded, a silent promise to himself.

Leon didn't protest as the man filled the doorway of his bedroom. He swiftly changed out of the hoodie and sweats into his work attire of well-cut black suit, black shirt, and tie. He held up his shoulder holster to the goon who nodded. Leon breathed easier. This *was* a business call. He sat on the bed, checked both his weapons, holstered them, then rolled on his socks and slipped into his boots.

He splashed his face and cleaned his teeth and looked

at himself in the mirror, seeing the strain in his cobalt blue eyes, and patted his face dry.

Marilyn breathed a sigh of relief as Leon rejoined her. "You look like you're going to a funeral," she muttered.

"You look smart," Acierno said unexpectedly. "Don Giovanni will appreciate that."

"What's he to you? Father, uncle?" Leon asked.

"Uncle. My pop's brother. The boys are my cousins." Acierno nodded at the goons.

Everything was kept in the family. Noted. Leon got to his feet. "Let's go."

Still at gunpoint, they led him and Marilyn to an armored SUV where he noticed a driver waited. Leon helped Marilyn into the back and Acierno sat on his other side, the goons facing them, Berettas on their laps.

They sat in silence, but Marilyn didn't let go of his hand as they traveled through the city toward her home. The SUV pulled up outside her single-story home with a neat front yard and bright red geraniums tumbling out of terra-cotta pots by the door.

Marilyn would never live there again. Leon would make sure of that.

Leon fixed his gaze on Acierno. "I'm taking her to the neighbors."

"The cops?"

Someone had done their homework.

"Yeah, the cops."

"You do right by us, and your sister will never see us again."

Leon said nothing. He trusted that promise about as far as he could throw the man mountain sitting opposite him.

He led Marilyn up the path to Frank and Jenny's door

and leaned on the doorbell. Their place was identical to Marilyn's, but with pots of herbs instead of flowers.

Frank opened the door. His ready smile for Marilyn faded when he saw how distressed she was and Leon, black-clad and grim-faced next to her. "What's happened? Is Noah all right?" Then he looked over their shoulders to the men in black standing by the SUV. "You in trouble, son?"

"I don't know," Leon admitted.

"Who are they?"

"Mafia. The Acierno family. I don't know what they want."

Frank's face tightened. He couldn't be a cop in the city and not know the Aciernos. "You're in trouble, Leon. I know them. They're bad news."

Leon nodded. Frank had been a cop his whole life. There wasn't much he didn't know about the city. Leon didn't want to talk about it in front of his sister. If, and it was a big if, he survived this encounter, he'd come talk to Frank and find out what he knew.

"I've gotta go. Take care of her."

Marilyn clutched onto him. "No, Leon, you can't go."

He unpeeled her fingers from his jacket and kissed her cheek. "I've got to, Maz." She shook her head. "For you and Noah." He pushed her over to Frank.

"She'll be fine with me and Jenny," Frank assured him, putting his arm around Marilyn's shaking shoulders.

Marilyn put a hand to her mouth and started to sob.

"Don't let her go alone to fetch Noah," Leon ordered. "You know who will be in touch."

Frank's face tightened again, and he gave a grim nod. Noah was the closest thing they had to a grandson. They wouldn't take kindly to the little boy being threatened. "They'll stay with us until then."

"Thanks." Leon shook Frank's hand and strode away to the sound of his sister dissolving into noisy weeping. He looked back at the men by the SUV and then at his sobbing sister. A white-hot anger burned inside him. They would pay.

He rejoined Acierno in the car and they drove away in silence.

Read Darker Daddy Bodyguards now

* * *

Click now to get my enemies-to-lovers adventure, Angel Securities, where Josh, Dominic and CDR make their appearance and the darker spin-off, Darker Daddy Bodyguards, with familiar faces.

* * *

About Sue Brown

Sue Brown is a Londoner with a dream to live on a small island. Coffee fuels her addiction to writing romance with hot guys loving each other, and her Adorkadog snores in harmony as she creates.

Love Sue's work? Support her at Ream. You'll get exclusive content and access to new books before anyone else.
You can find all of Sue's books over at her website.
Don't forget to sign up for her newsletter here.

Come over and talk to Sue at:
Sue's Subscribe: https://reamstories.com/suebrownstories
Newsletter: http://bit.ly/SueBrownNews
Bookbub: https://www.bookbub.com/profile/sue-brown
TikTok: https://www.tiktok.com/@suebrownstories
Her website: http://www.suebrownstories.com/
Author group – Facebook: https://www.facebook.com/groups/suebrownstories/
Facebook: https://www.facebook.com/SueBrownsStories/
Email: sue@suebrownstories.com